LOVELY BISCUITS

GRANT MORRISON

LOVELY BISCUITS
GRANT MORRISON

ISBN 1 902197 01 1
First published 1998 by
ONEIROS BOOKS
8 Short Street
Swansea
SA1 6YG
Tel / Fax 01792 472666

ACKNOWLEDGEMENTS;
"The Braille Encyclopaedia" first appeared in "Hotter Blood"
"The Room Where Love Lives" first appeared in 'Hottest Blood'
"Red King Rising" was first performed at the Netherbow
Theatre, Edinburgh on July 17 1989
Alice....Janet Dye
Dodgson....Christopher Craig
Directed by John Mitchell for Oxygen House
Designed by Bryan Angus
"Lovecraft In Heaven" first appeared in 'The Starry Wisdom'
"Depravity" was first performed at the Netherbow Theatre,
Edinburgh on August 16 1990
Directed by John Mitchell for Oxygen House
"I'm A Policeman" first appeared in 'Disco 2000'

ONEIROS

CONTENTS

for my Mum and Dad

INTRODUCTION

Recently there has been much talk of a "Scottish literary renaissance" and it is interesting that a number of extremely talented writers - including Grant Morrison, Frank Kuppner and Bridget Penney - have been largely ignored by the pundits promoting this idea. The neglect these writers have suffered at the hands of critical opinion is partially explained by the fact that their work simply doesn't dovetail with populist caricatures of Scotland as a place that is fundamentally romantic (to reuse the words of Fiona Macleod: "the Land of Youth, the shadowy Land of Heart's Desire").

While the novels of writers like James Kelman and Irvine Welsh are about as far away as you can get from clichés about the Scots being a nation of tartan clad rustics dwelling in misty glens or on craggy mountain peaks, their work can be read in ways that don't unsettle those reductive pastoral discourses which have long dominated both English literature and notions of what it is to be English and/or "British". While I'm not convinced that this is how either Kelman or Welsh intend their novels to be read, the notion of the "street" can be projected into their work and then substituted for the "peasant" croft as a repository of the "authentic" and "earthy wisdom".

Older critics who adopt the ruse I've just described tend to use the "street fictions" of Kelman and Welsh as a foil to play against a still dominant pastoral discourse. In style journalism, these reductive literary conventions are often blithely rewritten to fit a hackneyed "pop" agenda. Instead of being identified with the city, corruption is seen as emanating from those who are fat and old. In this barely revised scheme of things, youth is substituted for the countryside as a repository of "truth" and "innocence".

Trainspotting by Irvine Welsh was an important book because it changed industry perceptions about what could be successfully published. For these and other reasons Welsh is still seen as having a certain cachet and "credibility". Likewise, the demotic voicing of Welsh's English language fiction results in him being seen as quintessentially Scots. Other writers, such as Iain Banks and Martin Miller, have been exiled from much of the discourse about a "Scottish literary renaissance" precisely because they are perceived as being too popular, or at least too populist.

Grant Morrison finds himself in the almost unique position of being ignored by literary critics because his writing is both popular and self-consciously textual. The success of comics such as *The Invisibles* and *Dare* do not endear Morrison to those who believe that identities are simple constants rather than things that are endlessly remade. Morrison's blurring of boundaries between fiction and non-fiction, critical insight and satire, narrative and cyclical return, destabilise every category that conventional literary criticism is struggling to uphold.

There is no correct way to read Morrison, and different readers are making very different interpretations of his work. Personally, I believe that the pieces collected here are best read as an interconnected sequence despite their widely varying dates of composition. Taken alone, *Red King Rising* might be read as a defence of the romantic convention of prioritising the demands of the emotions over those of the intellect. Someone who took this view would have no difficulty in explaining why this encounter between Lewis Carroll and his 'fictional' creation Alice takes the form of what is - at least on the surface - a parody of Socratic dialogue. That said, a reading of this type is clearly undermined by the fact that children conventionally represent 'truth' and 'innocence', whereas throughout this piece Alice is portrayed as behaving in a 'calculated' manner.

Depravity offers itself less readily to traditional romantic readings than *Red King Rising*. As a "notorious" occultist, Aleister Crowley has been widely portrayed as a representative of intuition at war with intellect. In Depravity even Crowley's most irrational and obnoxious beliefs - such as his anti-Semitism - are depicted as weapons employed by cynical reason seeking its self-interested ends. Likewise, *I'm A Policeman*, lacks any obviously centred subject to constitute the "I" of the title. Anything might be playing the role of cop, from the dead labour embedded in commodities like "Diet Cloke", to the television or even "the country's greatest writer", who may or may not be the first person narrator. The reader is implicated whether they like this or not.

Had it not been published alongside *The Room Where Love Lives*, the story *Lovecraft In Heaven* might appear to be a straightforward example of inversion in which - "height of absurdity" - a famous horror writer rallies to the defence of reason and intellect. *The Room Where Love Lives* reads as if Clark Ashton Smith - one of the few writers to successfully combine satire and fantasy fiction - had decided weave into a single story tropes lifted from H. P. Lovecraft, Arthur Conan-Doyle and Samuel Delaney's *Tides Of Lust*. Parody and intertextuality spin off in so many directions that the reader is left completely at sea.

The Braille Encyclopaedia illustrates the impossibility of separating intellect from the senses, and thus the futility of theories that seek to privilege either reason or emotion. *The Story Of O* and Georges Bataille are clearly points of reference, but the ways in which they are meshed with post-modern concerns about the body and anti-ocular discourse create a dazzling sheen that defies interpretation. Morrison takes a perverse pleasure in upsetting expectations: best known for his work in the comics medium, he displays a keen interest in the anti-ocular; fascinated by psychogeography, the landscapes in this collection are obsessively textual. *The Braille Encyclopaedia* invokes a Paris self-consciously rendered as a literary abstraction, *The Room Where Love Lives* does the same for London.

Like Bridget Penney or Barry Graham, Morrison has been ignored by the pundits promoting the idea of a "Scottish literary renaissance" because his nomadic fictions endlessly reshuffle perspectives and locations. In both this and his concern with what has been termed "the politics of intellect", Morrison's work is far closer to that of the English vorticist Wyndham Lewis than any of the "canonical" works of the "Scottish literary renaissance". From certain twisted angles, Morrison's output exhibits a closer affinity to paradigmatic examples of modernism than the throughput of his romantically inclined "po-mo" contemporaries. For this, and much else besides, his texts merit considered reading.

STEWART HOME

THE BRAILLE ENCYCLOPAEDIA

BLIND IN THE CITY OF LIGHT, Patricia walked carefully back through the Cimitiere Pere-Lachaise.

"Are you all right?" Mrs Becque said again. "Now be careful here, the steps are a little slippery..."

Patricia nodded and placed her foot tentatively on the first step. Through the soles of her shoes she could feel the edge of a slick patch of moss.

"Are you all right?" Mrs Becque said again.

"I'll be fine," Patricia said. "Really."

All around, she could feel the shapes of sepulchres and headstones. The echoes they returned, the space they displaced, the subtle patterns of cold air they radiated; all these things gave the funeral monuments of Pere-Lachaise a weight and solidity that lay beyond sight. From the locked and chambered earth, a fragrance arose. The elaborate alchemy of decay released a damp perfume which combined with the scent of spoiled wreaths and hung like a mist around the stones. Rain drummed on the stretched skin of Patricia's umbrella.

"So what did you think?" said Mrs Becque. "Of Wilde's monument, that is? Did you like it?"

"Lovely," Patricia said.

"Of course, the vandals have made a terrible mess, writing all over the statue, but it's still very impressive, don't you think?"

Mrs Becque's voice receded into a rainy drone. Patricia could hardly mention how amused she'd been when she'd run her hands over Epstein's stone angel, only to discover that the balls of the statue had been chopped off by some zealous souvenir fiend. Mrs Becque would most certainly disapprove of so ironic a defacement, but Patricia felt sure that Oscar Wilde would have found the whole thing thoroughly entertaining. Mrs Becque, in fact, seemed to disapprove of almost everything and Patricia was growing desperately tired of the woman's constant presence.

"We must get in out of this awful rain," Mrs Becque was saying. They crossed the street, found a café and sat down.

"What would you like, dear?" asked Mrs Becque. "Coffee?"

"Yes," Patricia said. "Espresso. And a croissant. Thanks."

Mrs Becque ordered, then eased herself up out of her seat and set off in search of a telephone. Patricia took her book from her bag and began to read with her fingertips. She found no comfort there. More and more often these days, books did nothing but increase her own sense of isolation and disaffection. They taunted and teased with their promise of a better world but in the end they had nothing to offer but empty words and closed covers. She had grown tired of experiencing life at second hand. She wanted something that she had never been able to put into words.

A waiter brought the coffee.

"Something else for you, sir?" he said.

Patricia started up from her book. Someone was sitting at her table, directly opposite: A man.

"I'm fine with this," the man said. His voice was rich and resonant, classically trained. Every syllable seemed to melt in the air.

"I hope you don't mind," the man said. He was talking to Patricia now, using English. "I saw you sitting all alone."

"No. Actually, I'm with someone," Patricia said. She stumbled over the words, as she might stumble over the furniture in some unfamiliar room.

"She's over there. Over there." She gestured vaguely.

"I don't think you're with anyone at all," the man said. "You seem to me to be alone. It's not right that a pretty girl should be alone in Paris."

"I'm not," Patricia said flatly. The man was beginning to disturb and irritate her.

"Believe me," the man said. "I know what you want. It's written all over your face. I *know* what you want."

"What are you talking about?" Patricia said. "You don't know me. You don't know anything about me."

"I can read you like a book," he said. "I'll be here at the same time tomorrow, if you wish to hear more about the Braille Encyclopaedia."

"I beg your pardon?" Patricia's face flushed. "I really don't. . ."

"Everything all right, dear?"

Patricia turned her head. The voice belonged to Mrs Becque. Foreign coins chinked into a cheap purse.

"It's just this man. . ." Patricia began.

Mrs Becque sat down. "What man?" she said. "The waiter?"

"No. That man. There." Patricia pointed across the table.

"There's no one there, Patricia," Mrs Becque said using the voice she reserved for babies and dogs. "Drink up your coffee. Michel said he'd pick us up here in twenty minutes."

Patricia lifted her cup in numbed fingers. Somewhere the espresso machine sputtered and choked. Rain fell on the silent dead of Pere-Lachaise, on the streets and the houses of Paris, covering the whole city like a veil, like a winding sheet. . .

Patricia raised her head. "What time is it?" she said.

In her room, in the tall and narrow hotel on the Boulevard St Germain, Patricia sat listening to traffic. Outside, wheels sluiced through rain. Rain sieving down through darkness. Rain spattering on the balcony. Rain dripping, slow and melancholy, from the wrought-iron railing.

She sat on the edge of the bed, in the dark. Always in the dark. No need for light. The money she saved on electricity bills! She sat in the dark of the afternoon, ate another slab of chocolate and tried to read. It was hopeless; her fingers skated across the braille dots, making no sense of their complex arrangements. Unable to concentrate, she set her book down and paced to the window again. Soon it would be evening. Outside, in the dark and the rain, Paris would put on its suit of lights. Students would gather to argue over black coffee, lovers would fall into one another's arms. Out there, in the breathless dark and the flashing neon, people would live and be alive; and here, in this room, Patricia would sit and Patricia would read.

She sat down heavily and, unutterably miserable, slotted a cassette into her Walkman. Then she lay back on the bed, staring wide-eyed into her private darkness.

Debussy's "La Mer" began to play - the first wash of strings and woodwind conjured a vast and empty shore. White sand, desolate under a big sky. White waves smashed on the rocks. Patricia was writing something on the sand. Lines drawn on a great blank page of sand. She could not read what she was writing but she knew it was important.

Patricia licked dry lips, tasting chocolate.

What did he look like? The man in the café. The man with the voice. What would he look like if she could see him?

She unzipped her skirt and eased her hand down between her legs. The bed began to creak faintly, synchronising itself with Patricia's harsh, chopped breathing. . .

She was stretched out on watered silk in a scented room of flowers and old wine and he was there with his voice and his breath on her body his breath circulating in the grottoes of her ear and in her mouth and his skin and the mesh of muscles as he went into her

Debussy's surf broke against the walls of her skull. White wave noise drowning out the traffic and the rain, turning the darkness into incendiary light.

The music had come to an end. The room was too hot. An airless box. Patricia was suffocating in the dark. She rose, unsteadily, and faced the mirror's cold eye. She knew how she must look: a fat plain girl, playing with herself on a hotel bed.

"Stop it or you'll go blind," she said quietly. She felt suddenly sick and stupid. She would never meet anyone, never do or be anything. It all came down to this stifling room. No matter where she went, she found herself in this room. Reading. Always reading. Nothing would ever happen.

The dark closed in.

"I knew you'd be here," the man said. "I knew it."

"I don't see how you could just know," said Patricia and felt stupid. She was saying all the wrong things. `

"Oh, I know," he said. "I'm trained to recognise certain things in people. Certain possibilities. Certain. . inclinations." His hand alighted on hers and she jumped. "I can tell we're going to be friends Patricia."

"I don't even know your name," she said. She was becoming frightened now. She felt somehow that she was being circled. His voice was drawing a line around her. Sweat gathered between her breasts.

"My name?" He smiled. She could hear him smile. "Just call me L'Index."

"Sorry?" Patricia felt sure she must have misheard him. She tried not to be afraid. Being afraid was what had made her lonely.

"L'Index," the man repeated. "Like a book. L'Index."

"I can't call you that," Patricia said.

"You can: You must." He reached out and took her hand. It was like a soft trap, fastening around her wrist. "Dear Patricia. You must. You will. I will show you such things. . ." The fear was almost unbearable. She wanted to run. She wanted to go back. Back to that room, that book, like the coward she was. The man was holding open a door. Beyond lay darkness, it was true, but then again, Patricia was no stranger to the dark.

"L'Index," she said.

When Mrs Becque returned to the café to collect Patricia, Patricia had gone. One of the waiters had seen her leave with someone but found it impossible to describe the man. No one could describe the man. He had come and he had gone: a grey man in the rain.

Invisible. The police were alerted. Half-heartedly they scoured the city, then gave up. Patricia's parents mounted their own futile search. The newspapers printed photographs of a rather plump, blind girl, smiling at a camera she could not see. Her eyes were pale blue, their colour diluted to invisibility. Eyes full of rain, like puddles in a face. Very soon the papers and the public lost interest. Patricia's room lay untenanted. A stopped clock. The girl was never found and the police file stayed open, like a door leading nowhere.

The Chateau might have seemed like a prison were it not for the fact that it appeared to perpetually renew its own architecture. No door ever led twice to the same room, no corridor could ever be followed to the same conclusion, no stair could be made to repeat its steps.

Additionally, the variety of experiences offered by life in the Chateau was of such diversity that life outside could only be timid and pale by comparison. Here, there was no sin which could not be indulged to exhaustion. Here, the search for fresh sensation had long ago led to the practice of continually more refined atrocities. Here, finally, there were no laws, no boundaries, no limits, no judgement.

And the motto above the door read simply "Hell is more beautiful than Heaven."

Tonight was to be a special night. In the red room, in the room of the Sign of Seven, whose walls beat like a heart, Patricia lay in a tumble of silk cushions. She found a vein in her thigh and slowly inserted the needle. After the first rush, her head seemed to unlock and divide like a puzzle box. Her nervous system suffered a series of delicious shocks and smoke spilled into her brain. She licked red lips and began to shake.

into her brain. She licked red lips and began to shake. The tiny bells pinned to her skin reacted to her shudders. Her body became a tambourine. She drew a long breath. The room was hot and sweat ran on her oiled skin, trickling from the tongues of the lewd tattoos which now adorned her belly.

Above the pulse of the room, Patricia could hear the boy spitting, still spitting. L'Index had allowed her to touch the boy - to run her nails through his soft hair, to pluck feathers from the clipped and ragged wings he wore on his back and to finger the scars of his castration.

"What's he doing?" she said dreamily. "Why is he spitting?"

L'Index had come back into the room. He closed the door and waited for the boy to finish.

"He's been spitting into this glass," L'Index said. "Here."

Patricia took from him a beautiful crystal wineglass. L'Index knelt down beside her. Heat radiated off his body and he smelled faintly of blood and spiced sweat.

"The boy is an angel," L'Index said. "We summoned him here from Heaven and then we crippled and debauched him."

Patricia giggled.

"Our own little soiled angel," L'Index continued. "Come here, angel."

The boy shuffled across the room, slow as a sleepwalker. His wings rustled like dry paper.

"What shall I do with this?" Patricia asked, weighing the glass in her hand.

"I want you to drink it," L'Index said. "Drink."

Patricia dipped her tongue into the warm froth of saliva.

"He has AIDS, of course," L'Index said casually. "The poor creature has been the plaything of god knows how many filthy old whores and catamites. As you might expect, his spit is a reservoir of disease." He paused, smiling his almost-audible smile. "Nevertheless, I do insist that you drink it."

Patricia heard the boy whimpering as he was forced onto his hands and knees. She swirled the liquid round in the glass.

"Drink it *slowly*."

She heard the chink and creak of a leather harness. A match was struck. Was there no limit to what he would ask of her?

"All right," she said, nosing the glass like a connoisseur. It smelt of nothing. "I told you. I'll do anything."

And she drank, slowly, savouring the bland, flat taste of the boy's saliva. The whole glass, to the dregs. As she drank, she could hear the boy gasp - sodomised. Patricia licked the rim of her glass.

"You were lying," she said. "AIDS. I knew you were lying."

The boy cried out, with the voice of a bird. L'Index had done something new to him. Patricia waited for L'Index to undo the harness and sit down beside her.

"I knew I was right about you, when I saw you all those months ago," L'Index said. He tugged on the ring that was threaded through her nipple, pulling her toward him. Automatically, she opened her mouth and allowed him to place an unclean treat on her tongue.

"I knew you were worthy of admission."

"Admission?" said Patricia. "Admission into what?" The sound of her own voice seemed to recede and return. She was beginning to feel strange.

"Do you remember when I mentioned to you the Braille Encyclopaedia?" L'Index asked.

"Yes." Fragments of music flared in Patricia's head. Choral detonations. She felt that she was falling through some terrible space.

"The Braille Encyclopaedia. Yes. What is it?"

"Not a thing," L'Index said. "A society. Here. On your knees. Touch me."

He took her hand.

"But you've never let me. . ." she began, growing excited. White noise blasted through her, like a stereo pan, from ear to ear.

"I'm letting you now," he said. "You've shown a rare appetite for all the sweet and rotting fruits of corruption. Sometimes I'm frightened by your dedication. Now, I think it's time you were allowed to taste the most exquisite delicacy." He set her hand on his bare chest. Her fingers brushed his skin and she started.

"What is it?" Patricia lightly traced her fingertips across tiny raised scars. Alarm returned as she realised that his entire body, from neck to feet, was similarly disfigured. She ran along a row of dots, suddenly unable to catch a breath.

"It's braille," she said. "Oh, God, it's braille. . . I feel so strange. ." He filled her mouth and stopped her speech. Like a nursing child, she sucked and swallowed and allowed her hands to crawl across his skin.

"You drank angel spit," L'Index said. His voice was full of echoes and ambiguous reverberations. "You drank the rarest of narcotics. Now it's time to read me, Patricia. Read me!"

She read.

Entry 103   THE DEFORMATION OF BABY SOULS
Entry 45   THE HORN OF DECAY
Entry 217   THE MIRACLE OF THE SEVERED FACE
Entry 14   THE ATROCIOUS BRIDE
Entry 191   THE REGIMENTAL SIN
Entry 204   BLEEDING WINDO. .

Patricia snatched back her hand and pulled away, terrified. L'Index came into her face, spattering her useless eyes.

"What are you?" she whispered. She blinked and sperm tears ran down her cheeks. Somewhere, the fallen angel whimpered in darkness.

"There are several hundred of us," L'Index explained. "And together we form the most comprehensive collection of impure knowledge that has ever been assembled. Monstrous books, long thought destroyed, have survived as marks on our flesh. Through us, an unholy tradition is preserved."

"And what about me," Patricia said.

"One of our number died recently," L'Index said. "It happens of course, in the due process of time. Usually, we initiate a relative, often a child. My grandfather, for instance, was the Index before me. In this case, however, that was not possible. Part of my job is to find a suitable successor. . ."

Gripped by an extraordinary fear, Patricia dropped to the floor.

"Don't be afraid, Patricia," L'Index said: "Not you."

As she lay there, he pissed on her hair. She lifted her face into the hot stream, grateful for an act of degradation she could understand. It helped her to know he still cared.

"Will you abandon your last claim to self? Will you embrace the final release, Patricia? That is what I'm asking of you. Will you step over the threshold into a new world?"

"You sound like an evangelist," she said. His urine steamed in her hair. Patricia breathed deeply, inhaling a mineral fragrance. Slowly her heart rate came to match the pulsing of the room. She thought of what she had been and of what he had helped her become.

She held her breath for a moment. Counted to ten.

"Yes," she said hoarsely. `Yes."

They came singly, they came in twos and in groups: the Braille Encyclopaedia. Some were driven in black limousines with mirrored windows and no registration plates. Others walked, haltingly. Men, women, hollow-eyed children. They came from all directions, travelling on roads known only to a few mad or debased souls. They came and the doors of the Chateau opened to receive them. There was an almost electrical excitement in the air. The current ran through enchanted flesh, conjuring static in the darkness. Blue sparks played on fingertips as the Braille Encyclopaedia made its way into the Chateau. They were, each of them, blind, even the youngest. Silent and blind, blue ghosts, they entered the darkness. And the doors closed behind them.

Patricia did not hear them enter, nor did she hear L'Index welcome his guests. She sat in her chamber, listening to the fall of surf on an interior beach. On the bedside cabinets were vibrators, clamps, unguents, suction devices, whips: all the ludicrous paraphernalia of arousal. She was familiar with each and every item and she had endured or perpetrated every possible permutation of indecency that the body could endure.

Or so she had thought.

She touched her own smooth skin. She had removed the bells and the rings and towelled the oil away. Her skin was blank, like a parchment upon which L'Index wished to write unspeakable things. The music of Debussy crashed through her confusion.

We are all of us, she thought, written upon by time. Our skin is pitted and eroded by the passage of years. No one escapes. Why not then defy time by becoming part of something eternal? Why not give up all claims to individual identity and become little more than a page in a book which renews itself endlessly? It was, as L'Index had said, the final surrender.

Patricia removed her headphones and made her way downstairs.

L'Index was waiting for her and he introduced her to the members of the Braille Encyclopaedia. Blind hands stroked her naked body and, finding it unmarred, lost interest. She trembled as, one by one, they approached and examined her with a shocking frankness. Shameless fingers probed and penetrated her: the dry-twig scrapings of old men and women, the thin, furtive strokes of wicked children. By the end of their examination, Patricia teetered on the brink of delirium. Her darkness filled with inarticulate flashes and fireworks displays of grotesque colour and grossly ambiguous forms.

"They don't speak," she said. It seemed terribly important.

"No," said L'Index simply.

She felt them crowd around her in a circle, felt the pressure and the heat of unclothed flesh. No sound. They made no sound.

"Are you ready?" L'Index asked, touching Patricia's shoulder gently. She nodded and let him lead her into a tiny room at the back of the Chateau. Soundproofed walls. A single unshaded bulb, radiating a light she could not see. L'Index kissed her neck and instructed her not to move under any circumstances. She wanted to say something, but she was too afraid to speak. The words jammed at the back of her throat.

And then the door opened. Someone she did not know came into the room. Patricia suddenly wanted to run. The light was switched off and candles were lit, filling the room with a sickly sweet narcotic scent.

Patricia heard then a thin metallic ring. A sharp-edged sound. The brief conversation of scalpels and needles and blue-edged razors.

"L'Index?" she said nervously. "L'Index, are you there? I'm afraid. . "

No one answered. Patricia rocked on the balls of her feet. The air was too hot, the candle-smoke too bitter. She gulped lungfuls of oily, shifting smoke.
Someone came toward her, breathing harshly, sometimes mewing.

"L'Index?" she whispered again, so quietly that it was no more than the ghost of a name.

In her head, the noise and the colours mounted toward an intensity she felt she could not possibly bear.

The first cut caused her to spontaneously orgasm. Her brain lit up like a pinball machine. She swayed and she cried out but she did not fall as hooks and needles were teased beneath her skin. Moaning, coming again and again, Patricia was delicately scarred and cicatriced. Alone on a private beach, she realised what word it was that she had scrawled in the sand. And in that moment of understanding, the surf surged in and obliterated every trace of what she had written. Her identity was finally erased in the white glare of a pain so perfect and so pure that it could only be ecstasy. Fat, awkward Patricia was at last, at last, written out of existence by articulate needles.

She came to her senses and found that she was still standing. The spills of blood streamed down her body, pooling on the floor. She touched her stomach. The raw wounds stung but she could not help but run her fingertip along the lines of braille. She read one sentence and could hardly believe that such abomination could possibly exist let alone be described. Her whole body was a record of atrocities so rare and so refined that the mind revolted from the truth of them. How could things like this be permitted to exist in the world? She felt dizzy and could read no more.

"I'm still alive. I'm still alive," was all she could say. At last, she fell but L'Index was there to catch her.

"Welcome to the Encyclopaedia," he said, salting her wounds so that they burned exquisitely. "Now you are Entry 207 - The Meat Chamber."

She nodded, recognising herself, and he led her out of the room and down an unfamiliar corridor. She could feel herself losing consciousness. There was something she had to ask him. That was all she could remember.

"The Chateau," she said, slurring her words. "Who owns the Chateau?"

"Can't you guess?" L'Index said.

He brought her into the ballroom, where they were all waiting for her. Hundreds of people were waiting for her. She smiled weakly and said, "What now? Can I please sit down?"

"These gatherings happen only rarely," L'Index said. "The entire Encyclopaedia is not often assembled together in one place and so our lives take on true meaning only at these moments. I can assure you that what is about to follow will transcend all your previous experiences of physical gratification. For you, this will be the ultimate, most beautiful defilement. I promise."

He sat her down in a heavy wooden chair.

"I envy you so much," he said. "I'm only the Index, you see. The mysteries and abominations of the flesh are denied to me."

He pulled a strap across her arms, tugged it tight and buckled it.

"What are you doing?" she said. "Is this the Punishment Chair? It's not, is it?"

She began to panic now as he clamped her ankles to the legs of the chair. The Encyclopaedia was arranging itself into a circle again. Footsteps sounded down the corridor.

"This is the Chair of Final Submission," L'Index said. "Goodbye my love."

And he clamped her head back.

"Oh no," she said. "Wait. Don't. . ."

A clumsy bolt and bit arrangement was thrust into her mouth, chipping a tooth and reducing her words to infantile sobs and gobblings.

The footsteps advanced and the Encyclopaedia parted to make a passage. Shiny steel chinked slyly in a leather bag. L'Index leaned over and whispered in her ear.

"Remember, you may always consult me. . "

She bucked and slammed in the chair but it was fixed to the floor

by heavy bolts.

"Oh my sweet," L'Index said. "Don't lose heart now. Remember what you were: alone, lonely and discontented. You will never be lonely again." His breath stank of peppermint and sperm. "Now you can pass into a new world where nothing is forbidden but virtue."

A bag snapped open. A needle was withdrawn. It rang faintly, eight inches long.

"Give yourself up now to the world of the Braille Encyclopaedia! Knowledge shared only by these few, never communicated. Knowledge gained by sense of touch alone."

And she finally understood then, just before the needles punctured her ear-drums. Her bladder and her bowels let go and the odours of her own chemical wastes were the last things she smelled before they destroyed that sense also. Finally her tongue was amputated and given to the angel to play with.

"Now go," L'Index said, unheard. There was sadness in his voice. His tragedy was to be forever excluded from the Empire of the Senseless. "Join the Encyclopaedia."

Released from the chair, The Meat Chamber stumbled into the arms of her fellow entries in the Braille Encyclopaedia. Bodies fell together. Blind hands stroked sensitised skin. They embraced her and licked her wounds and made her welcome.

She screamed for a very long time but only one person there heard her. Finally she stopped, exhausted.

And then she began to read.

And read.
And read.

THE ROOM WHERE LOVE LIVES

It is with great regret that I commence this, the final account of my adventures with Aubrey Valentine. Readers who have followed the exploits of Aubrey Valentine from my first published account, *The Bleeding Whispers*, through to our most recent, *Mystery of the Flayed Mirror*, will be familiar with Valentine's singular skills in the field of occult investigation. I had hoped that our association would continue well into the future but, sadly, events have overtaken my wishes and it falls to me, as Valentine's chronicler, to bear the bad tidings to his many admirers.

So it is with heavy heart that I have assembled this final tale from the testimony of the Bedlow family, from Valentine's last statement, and from my own eyewitness account of the Monday Street horror. I can only pray that it will stand as a fitting tribute to the unusual life of the finest man I have ever known and one I was proud to call my friend.

The house on Monday Street was built late in the reign of Queen Victoria. A solid and imposing townhouse, it looked out across a quiet and tree-lined avenue in the heart of London. Almost as a reflection of the era of its construction, the house, while exhibiting a conservative, classical facade to the outside world, contained within its walls an eccentric profusion of rooms and chambers. Dusty alcoves below stairs gave onto narrow corridors connecting one room with another. There were secret rooms tucked away like forgotten unopened letters. Faded wallpaper in the basement, the attar of dead flowers, mirrors cataracted with thick dust.

And the house had passed through several hands before it became the property of a Dr. Bedlow and his family.

While it would not be true to say our story began with Mrs Bedlow and her daughter, it seems appropriate to begin the narrative with their unfortunate discovery of what we came to know as the Rutting Room.

Mrs. Bedlow had spent an afternoon shopping, at the close of which she collected her eighteen-year-old daughter, Imogen from the movies. Imogen's friend Giselle Barnes was to spend the evening with the Bedlows, and she accompanied them home in the car.

The girls hurried to Imogen's room, while Mrs. Bedlow went directly to the kitchen and dumped the contents of her bags onto the table.

A wedge of sunlight draped itself across table and floor like a flag, and Mrs. Bedlow paused to observe the dust motes moiling in the gauzy light. There was something unusual about the movement of the particles; they seemed to follow some subtle organising pattern. Like iron filings on paper, the dust motes arranged themselves into spiderweb formations. These then exploded, unable to sustain coherence, and were rearranged into new configurations. She admired this restless choreography for some time before the effect faded and it seemed as though her eyes had been deceiving her from the start.

She stocked the fridge and cupboards and prepared a snack for the girls. Carrying a small tray, she began to climb the stairs. Now she could feel a movement, a pulsation in the air. She touched the wall and her fingertips registered a deep, thudding concussion. It seemed as though the pipes beneath the skin of paper and plaster were pounding with a slow metronomic rhythm. She had a brief vision of gas mains, water pipes, and electric cable carrying arterial blood through the substructure of the house. The pulse quickened and Mrs. Bedlow felt her own heartbeat accelerate to match it. Sweat broke across her forehead and she was aware of a spreading dampness at her crotch, an involuntary, exciting, lubrication. She bit her lip and forced herself to the top of the stairs, reeling dizzily.

"Imogen," she said, and her voice was hoarse and breathless, pre-orgasmic. She had spoken her daughter's name as though it were the name of a lover. She approached the door of Imogen's room and stopped short.

The door handle was swelling and contracting slightly; inflating and deflating like a lung. And the sounds that came from beyond the door had no place in a girl's bedroom.

Slowly Mrs. Bedlow reached out to touch the keyhole. It was wet, leaking a musky sexual fluid. She raised her fingers to her lips and licked at them. She closed her hand around the warm, pulsing door handle and opened the door.

The whole room inhaled, drawing her into its suffocating heart. The smell of animals in heat. Smell of stained sheets and stale come and heated flesh.

"Look at me, Mummy," said Imogen, giggling.

She was bent over the bed, moaning and salivating. Giselle Barnes, kneeling, worked her hand between Imogen's legs. They both turned to look at Mrs. Bedlow, eyes heated to incandescence.

"Oh, God!" was the best Mrs. Bedlow could manage before the girls descended on her, tearing at her clothes.

There was a sustained note of shame in Mrs. Bedlow's voice as she recounted these events to us. That shame, quite clear in her words, was entirely absent in her demeanour. She sat in the kitchen, wearing a loose robe that was parted to reveal her pale body. Her legs were slung over the arms of a chair and she continued to masturbate slowly and compulsively as she talked. Sometimes she paused to wet her fingers in her mouth. She looked up at us with desperate eyes

"You must help as," she sobbed. "We can't stop it. We can't stop it, and my daughter's still up there." Then she seemed to lose control again, eyes closing. The rhythm of her hand became more insistent as she drifted into memory.

"It-was so beautiful." She sighed. "It was like she was trying to get back into my womb, headfirst. . "

Valentine eyed her coldly. I wondered if he ever experienced any human emotion now. I could not remember the last time I had seen him smile. He touched his brow with his bandaged left hand, always a sign that he was thinking deeply. There was silence, broken only by the chopped breathing of Mrs. Bedlow.

"Where exactly is your husband now, Mrs. Bedlow?" Valentine asked.

She jerked her head toward the ceiling. "With the girls. With *it*. He can't control himself. None of us can. The room just wants us to fuck and fuck until we die."

I looked at Valentine as he removed his duffle coat.

"I must examine the room before I make my decision," he said.

Mrs. Bedlow got to her feet I could see the dreadful exertion in her eyes. She was driven to seek sexual gratification by any means, and it clearly took a massive effort of will for her to restrain her urge to assault us.

"I'm frightened to go near it but I want to so much," she said. "It was only my husband who managed to push me out of the room on that first day. If he hadn't, I'd still be there."

Her hand crushed her breast, fingers teasing the swollen nipple. "I'd still be there."

"Quite," said Valentine curtly.

We climbed the stairs.

"Can you feel it?" Valentine hissed

I nodded. It was impossible not to be aware of the percussive thumping in the stairs below our feet. The room, whatever it was, had anchored itself deeply into the fabric of the house, extending roots into the infrastructure. Its power was unmistakable. My own pounding erection demonstrated that. I tried to imagine what it would be like to stay here night after night, as the Bedlows had done, slowly succumbing to that dreadful carnal hunger. I will never know how Mrs. Bedlow finally summoned the strength of will to contact Valentine and myself.

Mrs. Bedlow whined and whispered lewd endearments. Again I glanced in Valentine's direction, but his eyes were fixed on some unguessable horizon. I could not help but wonder how the power of the Rutting Room was affecting him. Since the horrible death of Angela, his young wife some years ago - as recounted in *The Affair of the Highgate Shroud* - he had been resolutely celibate, almost sexless indeed. Nothing could fill the gap Angela's death at the hands of The

Mysteries had left in his soul. If anyone could tackle the hideous sexual energies of this monstrous room, it was surely Aubrey Valentine.

"Here," said Mrs. Bedlow. She pointed to the door and backed away. Bracing her weight against the far wall; she selected a golf umbrella from the hatstand and slid the handgrip into herself. Weeping madly, bending and unbending her legs, she rode the wooden shaft. Her eyes clouded over. She crooned our names, begging us to join her.

"Poor Mrs. Bedlow," I muttered, trying to push away the thoughts that bubbled into my mind.

Valentine ignored her cries and faced the door.

"Are you ready?" he said. I nodded, unsure, and he motioned for me to stand behind him. He reached out and gripped the door handle. It stiffened in his grip, becoming tumescent. Without further hesitation, he threw the door open and we confronted the room.

The first thing was the smell: a vast reeking perfume that spoke of reeling, desperate nights and polluted innocence. It was the bleak perfume of all blighted desire. This first olfactory shock was followed by the visual horror. The scene within the room recalled some image from Bosch.

Giselle Barnes in the soiled tatters of her dress, was servicing three naked men. Imogen Bedlow giggled and drove a policeman's baton repeatedly into her own bleeding anus. As we watched, the tableau collapsed and its elements reformed. Now the men were locked in a knot of buggery and felatio, while the girls sucked and tore at one another.

Valentine gestured to one of the men. "Bedlow?" he said.

I nodded.

Imogen, on all fours, backed up and impaled herself on her father's penis. The eminent Dr. Bedlow gripped the girl's shoulders and pulled her back roughly. At one point, he managed to turn his head to face us. There were tears in his eyes. "God help me," he cried, and before he could say anymore, one of the other men mounted him from the rear.

"It's monstrous," I said. It was monstrous, but I could not deny the black excitement I felt.

"But look there," said Valentine, pointing upward. The walls of the room were shifting through strange geometric patterns. I felt I was watching some nightmarish four dimensional origami at work on the architecture of the place. The patterns on the wallpaper flowed into suggestive shapes. Wet slits opened in the walls, gaped, and were sealed.

And at that moment the door slammed shut in Valentine's face. He produced a kitchen towel from his pocket and wiped his brow.

"Who are the other men?" he said calmly.

Mrs. Bedlow looked up from the floor. "Giselle's father," she said. "And a policeman. They were all trapped there."

Then, unable to retain restraint, she withdrew the umbrella handle and rubbed her wet thighs with her hands, baying "Fuck me!" again and again and again.

Valentine strode toward her and, with one precise movement, rendered her unconscious. Then he slung her over his shoulder and we left the house.

We were in our room at the YMCA and Mrs. Bedlow sat drinking instant coffee. Soberly dressed now, there was scarcely anything about her that recalled the nymphomania of several hours previously. Nevertheless, she appeared to be in deep shock. The heat had gone from her eyes, leaving a glassy blankness.

"What are we going to do about my daughter?" she said.

"When was your last period?" Valentine said.

Mrs. Bedlow looked up from her mug, frowning.

"Months," she said. "I thought it was another baby."

"I doubt very much that you're pregnant, Mrs. Bedlow. I believe that the room induced in you and your daughter and the Barnes girl a state of super-receptivity. It made you like itself, a fucking machine, unable to orgasm or to replicate. Coitus for its own sake."

She began to sob, and I reached out to take the coffee mug from her numb fingers.

"What *is* it, Mr. Valentine?" she said. "What is it? What's it doing to my daughter?"

Valentine ignored the question, perhaps not daring to tell her the truth.

"What do you know of the history of the house, Mrs. Bedlow?"

She dabbed at her eyes with a tissue. "Not much. Before we moved in, it belonged to some old woman. Her son said something about it being a kind of private hospital before that. A clinic or something. That's all I know. If there was anything else. . ."

"Stop!" Valentine said abruptly. I could see he was onto something. "Monday Street. Of course! I knew I recognised the name." He turned to face me. "There's a book in my large suitcase," he said. "*Cults of the Pandemonium*. Would you be so kind as to fetch it for me?"

I threw open the battered valise and rummaged through a debris of dog eared paperbacks, quickly locating *Cults of the Pandemonium*. Its luridly coloured cover depicted a gorgeous naked hermaphrodite dancing, while a shadowy figure beat upon a tom-tom. I tossed the book to Valentine and he flipped through its pages.

"I should have known!" he said. His eyes scanned a page. "Erich Horney. My God. Horney was a disciple of Wilhelm Reich. He worked at the Organon Institute in Maine in the late '40s, before splitting with Reich in 1952."

We listened intently as Valentine summarised a brief biography of the aptly named Horney. He had adapted many of Wilhelm Reich's sexual theories and taken them in unusual and, some thought, unethical directions.

"His dream was to create something that he called the Horney Chamber," Valentine explained. "This seems to have been a more extravagant version of Reich's orgone accumulator. Basically, Horney intended to create a room which could harness sexual energy, which he believed was an expression of the fundamental forces of the universe. "As he spoke, Valentine paced up and down the room.

"He claimed to have succeeded in building a prototype in 1965, but its development was hampered by the fact that the room's mechanisms could only be properly activated by an act of indefinitely long sexual intercourse. Nevertheless, by judiciously employing four porno actors, Horney claimed that his chamber was able to absorb and redirect sufficient sexual energy to power the flight of a small gargoyle-like homunculus.

"His ultimate ambition was to create a room which could have sex with *itself*, thus producing an unlimited supply of power. A perpetual-motion sex engine."

Valentine threw down the book and looked directly at us. His face was flushed with excitement.

"Horney was certified insane in September 1974 and was taken into the private care of a Dr. Monteuil, who owned a small convalescent clinic on Monday Street."

"Good Lord!" I exclaimed, unable to think of else to say.

"And the room?" Mrs. Bedlow said. "My daughter's room?"

"I think we can safely assume that a fully functioning Horney Chamber was built, Mrs. Bedlow. Perhaps Horney died before he could put the room into operation and it has waited all these years for a trigger. Something to turn the starting handle, as it were."

He paused and lifted his bandaged hand to his brow.

"Does your daughter have a boyfriend, Mrs. Bedlow?" he asked.

She nodded, realising the implications. "It's not what you'd call serious," she said. "They met on a school trip to Belgium. They exchange letters. . ."

"There we have it," Valentine said gravely. "Those nocturnal adolescent yearnings: our trigger."

"But what can we do?" Mrs. Bedlow said. "How can we stop it?"

Valentine sat down facing her and took her hands. He fixed her eyes with his own.

"I haven't told you everything, Mrs. Bedlow;" he said.

I felt a tremor trip down my spine. The sky outside our room seemed to thicken. Shadows curdled in the haunted corners of our anonymous chamber.

"There are certain powers and dominions in our universe;" Valentine said. "I can say only that they come from *outside* and that they are inimical to humanity. Sometimes we catch glimpses of their manifestations on this plane of being. They travel in many shapes, all hideous. They come howling through our blackest dreams, feeding on our fears and doubts.

We call them The Mysteries, and I have dedicated my life to fighting them. They destroyed the only woman I have ever cared for, and now they have taken possession of the activated Horney Chamber. They will try to use its energies to create a window, through which they can enter our world *en masse.*"

"But my daughter. . ." Mrs. Bedlow began. Valentine silenced her with a gesture.

"Your daughter, your husband, and the others are nothing more than raw material to The Mysteries," he said. "They will use them to destruction in order to power the room. When they have exhausted all the possible combinations of the human frame, The Mysteries will push them beyond the limits of flesh. They will become expressions of pure desire, without stable form."

Mrs. Bedlow was sobbing uncontrollably now, and she managed to say only six words: "What are we going to do?"

Valentine stood up.

"You're going to stay here, well away from the house," he said, and then looked at me. "We are going to take the fight to The Mysteries."

I think I will always remember Valentine the way he was at that moment. It is the picture of him that I will carry with me to the grave: Valentine, framed by the window, cast like a statue in shadow and light. His hawklike, scarred face, his leonine hair, his angular shoulders bent with a burden of melancholy. This memory remains clear, like a snapshot of a long-lost perfect day. And, in my mind, he will never fade nor grow old.

Let's go," said Valentine, picking up his bag.

The light inside the house had taken on a curious red cast. The air had congealed into a bloody miasma that caught in the back of the throat and reeked of sweat and sex.

"Will we be strong enough to fight it?" I asked. Already my penis was knocking against the door of my trousers, stiffening into a club. I found myself watching Valentine's buttocks shift under his jeans.

"This is only a residual effect," he said: "The real power is in the room itself. It's anchored itself to the house. In order to function more efficiently as a gateway for The Mysteries. We must prevent that from happening."

As we climbed the stairs, the sound of the room became louder. It was moaning. A deep bass note vibrated through the walls and floor.

"I'm afraid, Valentine," I admitted. "I can feel itself insinuating its way into me. What if I can t control myself?"

"Then try to enjoy it," he said grimly.

We stood outside the door: Valentine reached into his bag and transferred a number of items to his pockets. Finally, he selected a brace of Band-Aids from a silver plated tin.

"I'll be looking beyond the real," he said. "You must be my eyes if I need a description of events on this plane." Thus saying, he fixed the strips of sticking plaster over his eyelids.

I wiped my brow and picked up Valentine's bag.

"Ready?" he said, and, before I could reply, the door was open and we were swept into the Bacchanal.

The first thing I saw was the young policeman. His body was no longer his own and had become a mere engine of unfocused lust. The Mysteries had worked their enchantments upon his flesh and transformed it to suit their own ghastly purpose. His body seethed, like a bag of skin filled with serpents. Mouth and nose were fused into a single glistening slit with staring eyes on either side. His eyebrows had grown together into a thick pubic mass at the crown of this rudimentary vagina. His tongue thrashed from his transformed face, flicking thick liquid onto the bodies of his fellow revellers. Heavy extrusions surged out of the young policeman's torso, searching for receptive orifices before subsiding back into his rippling musculature. His penis was extended, fractal-branching into a cat-o'-nine tails that flailed and penetrated men and girls and the very walls of the room with indiscriminate abandon.

Giselle was pounding her fist repeatedly into a gaping, flaming hole at the base of the policeman's spine. When I caught a closer glimpse of the girl's hand, I realised that it too had suffered a monstrous transformation, becoming a blunt, glistening phallus. The other men and Imogen were not so radically altered, but I could not help but be aware of the way in which their skin seemed to slide and flow.

This, then, was the scene that greeted me when I entered the room. I will not lie; I wanted to retch, but at the same time I was stimulated to the threshold of my self-control. Here was pure flesh, pure desire, set free from all restraint and given uninhibited expression. All the impulses that drive the human animal were here distilled and unleashed.

The room itself was no less active than its occupants. Every object strained at the limits of its construction. Chairs, tables, toys, furnishings: All these things ached with a newly revealed eroticism; each attempting to form of its substance some representation of cunt or cock. The walls, floor and ceiling were alive. Suffused with a rosy glow, they extended stalagmite dildoes upon which the occupants of the room pleasured themselves. Vibrating gashes blinked open in the walls, eager to be filled.

My mind and body reeled, and I could no longer tell whether I was in Hell or in Heaven.

I glanced at Valentine blindly surveying the room and tried to describe what I was seeing. I knew that he saw something quite different. His "sealed vision" permitted him to penetrate to the normally veiled essential nature of things. He saw the naked room.

"My God! I heard him say: "The taint runs deep. . ,"

He raised his bandaged hand toward the tall, narrow windows on the far side of the room. I forced myself to look beyond the carnal chaos to those open windows. The scene there bore no relation to the cityscape one would have expected to see from that perspective. Instead of chimneys and treetops and clouds, I found a nocturnal sky, filled with liquid stars. Silhouetted against these dream constellations, I discerned vast structures. The windows of these threatening buildings were lit with a whole new spectrum of unearthly colours. The buildings spat vast streamers or aurorae into the sky, and I heard sounds I cannot explain. For just a moment, it seems, I was granted a vision of a world beyond known philosophies. A world where amniotic seas raged through living cities.

"What is that place?" I said. "What are those buildings?"

"They're not buildings," Valentine said, and he began to unwrap the stained bandages that covered his left hand.

It pains me to confess that; at that moment, I lost all control. Something pushed me back and I fell. The room roared and fluxed around me and I raised my head to see Imogen Bedlow's lips fastened around my erection. I slid in and out of her mouth and could feel strange cold spaces at the back of her throat. As she gorged herself on me, her own father took her from behind and, almost as quickly, Barnes was upon *me*. Worse was to follow as I helped him to divest me of my clothing. With writhing, lactating nipples, he fell upon me and drove himself into me. I abandoned myself to the delirious, monotonous rhythm of the bewitched room.

Giselle and the young policeman seemed to be fusing together somewhere in the centre of the room, creating a new and fabulous organism. I saw a shrieking, deformed thing rearing up toward the ceiling and collapsing like a wave. It was beautiful and glorious, a living Henry Moore sculpture carved from bleeding flesh. It strained for heights of gratification I could scarcely imagine, and I watched it pass into the palpitating substance of the room itself Then I collapsed, hovering on the brink of orgasm for what seemed like endless hours.

Suddenly Imogen was torn away from me. I looked up through a red fog to see Valentine pushing her back against the wall. She tongued the air, pleading with him to abuse her. Calmly, Valentine removed a key from his pocket and placed it in the girl's mouth. Her eyes closed in bliss and she began to suck on the rusty key. Valentine ignored the hands that scrabbled at the zip of his trousers and turned the key in Imogen's mouth. I swear that I heard the clacking sound of an ancient lock. Imogen's eyes snapped open, like switch- blades. She began to scream.

For a moment, the spell was broken. Barnes and Bedlow pulled away from one another in disgust and horror.

"Get them out of here!" Valentine shouted. I tugged at my trousers and tried to restore some dignity to my appearance.

"Forget your trousers!" he cried. "Just get them out!"

Ignoring my nakedness, I managed to push the others out of the room and onto the landing.

I paused at the threshold and turned. Valentine lifted his uncovered left hand. It was withered horribly, like the hand of some mummified king. This, I knew, was another legacy of his most dreadful confrontation with The Mysteries. Angela had died and Valentine had lost the use of his hand. It had, however, become for him a potent object of power. He placed birthday-cake candles on the tips of each finger and lit them. Then he lifted his Hand of Glory in preparation for the final battle.

"Valentine; for God's sake!" I whispered. "You can't fight them alone."

"I'm not alone," be said. "Get out now, while you still can! The only way to stop them is to use the room's own power. It'll destroy you if you stay."

The air was filling with strange viscous streamers. Pearly-white, like semen floating free of gravity, this substance filled the air around us. Thin tendrils glistened and sang.

"They're coming!" he said.

"I can't leave you too fight them alone. . ." I tried to say again.

"Out!" he yelled, and the door blew shut in my face.

"May God help you, Valentine," I whispered.

There was a moment of calm in which I heard Imogen Bedlow weeping softly, and then a surge of power shook the walls and I was thrown down the stairs.

I recovered my senses to see Barnes and Bedlow kissing passionately on the landing. Imogen crawled between their writhing bodies, licking and sucking at whatever she could find. Eventually she sandwiched herself in such a way that both men could fuck her simultaneously. I struggled with the urge to join them.

There was a great ululating sound from the Rutting Room and I ran back up the stairs. I could not leave Valentine to his fate. With shaking hands, I opened the door for the last time.

Of Giselle Barnes and the young policeman, no evidence remained, except for a shuddering cube of stressed flesh.

Valentine hung suspended and naked in the centre of the room, thrashing at the heart of a twitching web, a great spidery crucifixion. Filaments and protrusions extended from every corner of the room to penetrate his mouth and rectum. His pelvis bucked and his penis slammed like a piston in and out of a soaking orifice that the room had manufactured for itself.

"Valentine!" I shouted, but he did not respond.

His body spasmed automatically. The far wall no longer existed, and in its place then was a vista of staggering abnormality, through which those monstrous "buildings" came lurching. Faces were scorched into walls. Leering, childish drawings appeared and were erased by unseen hands. The word "SUBMISSION" was scrawled with some diarrheal substance that faded into bilious smoke. Saliva ran from the walls. I felt that I was simply an observer in the midst of a battle I could not comprehend.

I looked up to see Valentine extend his Hand of Glory. The tiny candles flared and shredded paper began to rain down from the ceiling: The room's breathing grew more rapid and the walls flushed red. The same colour spread across Valentine's skin like a rash. His own breathing was synchronised with that of the room. Together they ascended toward some unendurable climax. The Mysteries reached into the room, spreading a scabbed, diseased shadow across the windowsill.

There was one ineffable moment when everything paused at once, and then Valentine threw back his head and screamed.

It is to my eternal shame that I fled from the room and did not stay to help my friend. Instead, I joined Barnes, Bedlow and Imogen for a final mesmeric orgy. Her bruised lips locked about me and I was lost.

When I awoke from my wet dream, it was to find Valentine standing over me. The fingertips of his left hand were charred to matchsticks.

"I'm sorry. ." I began.

"It's all right," he said: "They're gone, for now, and there was nothing you could have done to help. That door has been sealed forever. "

"Thank God," I muttered. The unconscious bodies of my recent lovers lay tangled on the floor. "What have I done?"

Valentine shook his head. "More lives destroyed by those monsters!"

"But what about you?" I said.

He simply turned and walked back toward the door that opens onto the Horney Chamber. At the threshold, he paused and looked down.

"When Angela died, I thought *I* had died to love," he said. "I was cored, hollowed-out. Now it seems I've found the thing that was lost to me."

"The room?" I said, barely articulating the words.

He nodded. "I was enflamed," he said quietly. "I transformed the room into an instrument of purest love. The carnal and the spiritual united. The Mysteries had managed to pervert the room's true inclinations. I restored them."

I knew then what he was about to say.

"The Horney Chamber; powered by love; opens out into innumerable worlds. It can be folded through dreams, into unimaginable universes," he said. "Rainbow skies and blue, raging storms of tear-stained love notes. It's all out there, old pal."

He smiled at me. "That's where I'm going."

He reached out and laid his ruined hand on my shoulder.

"Goodbye," he said.

He opened the door. From within, I heard the sound of a great sighing. The room was filled with light; spring mornings and new rain, scented black chiffons, red lamps swinging in the sweat of the night. All the colours of desire, all love and longing expressed in one eloquent rush of charmed air.

"Goodbye, Aubrey," I said.

And Aubrey Valentine stepped into the room where Love lives and closed the door, and I never saw him again.

RED KING RISING

CHARACTERS

ALICE - arrogant yet naive Victorian upper class child. There is, however, the constant impression that she is conscious of playing a role. There is a certain calculated nature in everything she says and does. Not too overt.
LEWIS CARROLL - Almost more of an idea, an attitude, than a real man.

The key to the performance should be barely suppressed rage, hysteria and paranoiac bitterness. Carroll is a kettle on the boil, sometimes exploding, always simmering.

(Darkness. Victorian London ambience: rattle of cartwheels, clatter of hooves on cobbles. A churchbell begins to sound the hours. On the heels of each stroke of the bell, a red light flashes, synchronised with the funereal bell-sound to create a rhythm which is close to that of a beating heart - bell/flash, bell/flash..
The stage is bare but for the chalked outline of a murder victim - splay of limbs in death posture - Catherine Eddowes, fourth victim of the Whitechapel Ripper.
On the fifth stroke of the bell, a girl appears - ALICE - dressed for Wonderland. She moves around tentatively, caught in the pulsed red light like a spirit new to hell. She almost steps into the chalk outline but catches herself on the brink. She examines the outline.
The bell strikes twelve. The sound fades but the red light remains. ALICE stands still. Only her head moves as she looks up and around. London street noises fade up slowly, then fade down as the light changes, shifting away from the

red. A light, mysterious and bluish, suggestive of night, takes
the place of the red glow.

ALICE waits. A beat. Two.

ALICE sets a finger to her lips.)

ALICE: SHH! London is asleep. England is asleep.
All the judges and the bishops, all the lords and
ladies and the old governess, her Majesty the
Queen (*She curtsies, mockingly.*) they're all tucked
up in their beds tonight. I used to wonder what
they dreamt about but now I think I know. I
think that when they dream they dream this..

(Looks up and around.)

All day long in starched collars, buttoned to the
throat. All day long, pulled into whalebone stays
and tied tight. All day long in the bright light of
the glorious Empire... And at night, when they're
asleep, they creep through the streets of
Whitechapel, through the fog and gaslight, like
shadows..

(Suddenly brisk, matter-of-fact.)

Anyway, that's what I think. You needn't think
anything of the sort. That's one of the rules
children ought never to forget - other people's
ideas are very often bad for you. Similarly, a red
hot poker will burn you if you hold it too long; if
you cut your finger very deeply with a knife, it
usually bleeds and if you drink much from a

bottle marked 'poison', it is almost certain to disagree with you sooner or later.

CARROLL: 'Away fond thoughts and vex my soul no more!

Work claims my wakeful nights, my busy days.

Albeit bright memories of that sunlit shore Yet haunt my dreaming gaze.'

(As he speaks, LEWIS CARROLL, emerges from the darkness, wearing gloves. He reads from 'Alice's Adventures in Wonderland' He completes the verse and ALICE claps her hands. CARROLL casually tosses the book away, smiles indulgently.)

CARROLL: Thank you. I couldn't help but overhear you mention a red hot poker. That reminds me of a rather amusing story concerning Edward the Second of England.

ALICE: A story, Mr. Dodgson! ....

CARROLL: Carroll! Mister Carroll! I'm Lewis Carroll not Dodgson! Oh no, old Reverend Dodgson's fast asleep in his cold bed. Fast asleep and dreaming me!

ALICE: That seems to prove a theory of mine.

CARROLL: What? Little girls don't have theories! In fact, little girls don't have much of anything, really. That may be why I find them so.. so.. let's just say 'stimulating' and perhaps I can continue to avoid arrest.

(As he speaks, CARROLL, walks around ALICE, predatory, barely restraining a paedophiliac lust. His hands caressing the air around her.)

To me, a little girl is like a blank sheet of paper, just begging to be written on..

(He mimes writing his name upon her body. She looks a little anxious.)

..to be scrawled over like a private diary..

(ALICE side-steps and briskly changes the subject.)

ALICE: So, Mr. Dodgson won't be along then?

CARROLL: No. He won't be along and that's the long and the short of it. If I could ban him completely from my life, I would do it, believe me. Have you ever read any of his books? 'The Fifth Book of Euclid treated Algebraically, so far as it Relates to Commensurable Magnitude'! It hardly leaps off the shelf now, does it?
I don't know what he'd have done without me. I made him! And he denied me! As Peter denied Christ, Dodgson denied Carroll. Cock-a-doodle-do! Three times...

ALICE: It seems very sad that there are to be no more 'Alice' stories. I feel like a stopped clock. What will I do with my time now?

CARROLL: I didn't say there were to be no more 'Alice' stories. Did I say that? All I said was that Dodgson refused to write anymore. He didn't dare write another 'Alice' for fear of what it might reveal about him. The photographs were bad enough, for God's sake! Anyway, he felt he'd said his grand farewell in 'Through the Looking Glass'. Do you remember? When Dodgson himself, in the guise of the White Knight, said goodbye to Alice and rode off into a sunset the colour of fresh blood. Alice skipped off to become a Queen, to get married, to have children of her own and to forget the miserable old bastard who loved her, who wanted to tear off her knickers..

ALICE: Mr. Carroll!

CARROLL: But couldn't even bring himself to touch her. In the book, as in life, Alice took the place of the Red Queen. Red for spilled blood. Very significant.

ALICE: Poor Mr. Dodgson.

CARROLL: Weak. That's all. Alone in his dark room, in the red light. Alone with his photographs and his memories. So, I said to him, 'One more 'Alice,' I said. 'Go on, write one more and set yourself free.' But there was no-one to tell the story to. No-one who would listen without judging him mad or worse.

(He takes her hands. Simpering Carroll begging for understanding. They kneel down together in the spreading golden light.)

ALICE: No more rowing boats on the Thames.

CARROLL: No. Oxford seems like a dream to me now. Those long days of cut grass. The sun in the evening and the great slow fall of light on the stones and the spires. The Dreaming Spires. We're far from the Golden Country now, you and I..

The last thing I wrote for Dodgson was 'The Hunting of the Snark'.

ALICE: But what about the final 'Alice'?

CARROLL: Dodgson couldn't write it. He couldn't face the hideous truth of the bloody thing. In his terror, he expelled me. Left me to my own devices, you might say.

ALICE: And?..

CARROLL: And I wrote the story myself. It's all here.

(Taps head.)

Scribbled across the old grey matter. All I need is someone to tell it to.

(CARROLL looks at ALICE, sizing her up.)

An eager listener.

ALICE: So, there really is a new 'Alice' after all?

CARROLL: Yes. The final adventure. The secret 'Alice'.
I call it 'Alice in the Labyrinth'.

ALICE: How wonderful!

CARROLL: It's based on the Game of Goose and on the
initiatory Labyrinth of Crete.

(ALICE sits down, cross-legged, to listen.)

ALICE: I've never cared for Greek..
(CARROLL indulges in a private joke.)

CARROLL: Dodgson never cared for Greek either.
However...the story begins with Alice, thirteen
years old and no longer a child. The setting is
Christ Church, Oxford. Alice reluctantly takes
leave of her companion - a young county
cricketer named Hargreaves - and hurries off to
visit a dear friend of many years. The friend is
Dodgson, a mathematics don. A C of E deacon
with a tuh-tuh-tuh-terrible stammer.

(ALICE laughs with recognition at the imitation.)

Alice creeps into Dodgson's rooms and is
shocked to find him on the floor. He lies naked,
surrounded by torn photographs of little girls,
scattered playing cards and disarrayed chess
pieces. His mouth -

(Draws hand across lips.)

- closed with sealing wax. His eyes, staring.

Alice kneels down beside him and whispers in his ear.

ALICE: Oh, Mr. Dodgson.. I'd have let you if you'd wanted..

CARROLL: But it's his deaf ear and the words come straight back out again in reverse order.

ALICE: ..wanted you'd if you let have I'd.. Dodgson Mr. Oh

CARROLL: And so, Alice picks up her skirts and jumps into Dodgson's ear. Into that great well of an ear which suddenly rises up all around her, red walls all aglow with capillary blood, a spiralling tunnelful of interesting words which have been caught there like flies on paper.
And as she falls, Alice reaches out and plucks a word.

ALICE: Puberty.

(Alice makes a face, spits with disgust.)

CARROLL: She tries it in her mouth but the taste is so horrible that she has to spit the word out.

(ALICE looks at CARROLL. A sneaking, 'You've got a guilty secret' look.)

ALICE: Pae-do-

CARROLL: *(Hastily butts in.)* But that word is too big to fit in her mouth, so she throws it away too.

ALICE: So many words. Down. Down. Down. A whole dictionary of trapped and useless words.

CARROLL: Would the fall never come to an end?
At length, her skirts open like a bell and she drifts down, down, dandelion down, like seed on the wind, until her feet touch solid ground and she stands at the door to the Labyrinth.

ALICE: Is it a maze, like Hampton Court?

CARROLL: Hampton Court, like every other maze that ever was, is no more than a crude copy of this maze. For this is the original maze. The interior labyrinth. The human brain. A house divided.
Not at all cautiously, for she never was a cautious child, Alice enters along the spinal corridor into the brainstem.

ALICE: Guarded by crocodiles, I see.

CARROLL: Crocodiles in pinstripes. Now Alice must wade through a pool of crocodile tears. Sweet and salty. Buoyant as the Dead Sea.

ALICE: How strange! It looks like water but it isn't wet!

CARROLL: That's because crocodiles can't really cry.

ALICE: If I continue, how will I ever remember the way back?

CARROLL: You can wind out the silver thread of your life, just as Theseus unravelled the ball of golden twine to mark his passage through the Cretan Labyrinth, in search of the Minotaur. But remember! Your life has been short and the thread may not stretch far enough.

ALICE: Oh, I'm sure length isn't everything..

(ALICE points to the chalk outline on the floor.)

What's this? A puzzle?

CARROLL: I suppose. A puzzle solved perhaps. A line chalked round the body of a murdered woman. A victim of the Minotaur. You can still see the bloodstains. Look!

ALICE: Poor thing.

CARROLL: Poor exactly. I expect she was some dizzy whore with bad breath and crabs. The streets are full of them. Trying to make ends meet. She's better off on a mortuary slab, keeping someone busy.
See how they've caught the attitude of her limbs! She's lucky someone cared enough to immortalise her in chalk. This is what a human life looks like stripped down to the basics. This is that woman reduced to lines, reduced to a pure geometry. Her life story simplified into one essential pictogram. Dodgson would love it. He'd write some unreadable book about vectors

and logarithms and it would end up on a second hand stall in Farringdon Road.

(Pauses to regard the outline once more.)

Who'd imagine the old slag could end up looking so pure? No painting could have flattered her that way. No photograph. Look at her! She looks like the map of an imaginary country or a letter from some exotic alphabet.

ALICE: I think she looks rather sad. I think it's wrong that people should be poor at all.

CARROLL: You're right. There should be no poor. We must find a way to do away with the poor altogether. Send the men off to war and slaughter the women back home. Off with their heads! Ideally, we could reduce them all to white lines like this.. magic them all into numbers, into...statistics, shall we say? Yes. We shall. Make them all vanish by some mathematical sleight of hand.

ALICE: Can I move on now? I'm anxious to avoid this Minotaur if I possibly can.

(CARROLL ignores her, preoccupied.)

CARROLL: Ah, but where would we be without the poor?

(He climbs up, overlooking the stage.)

How high could the rest of us climb if it weren't for the shoulders of the poor on which we stand? Answer me that?

ALICE: Is this another riddle?

CARROLL: I'm speaking rhetorically now. I'm playing the Devil's Advocate. Bible bashing Dodgson would doubtless disagree but I think the work of Mr. Darwin bears me out here. The doctrine of natural selection suggests that the strongest and most ruthless are the ones who rise. The weak are justly destroyed by their own lack of willingness to adapt. That's science, that is, and who are we to argue with the facts?

(Alice joins Carroll and they both survey the stage, as from a balcony.)

And here we are. How small they all look! This is how the Queen herself must feel, don't you think? This is how dear old Victoria - God bless her! - must feel on her throne. Squatting over her subjects and dropping the odd shit onto their upturned faces. That's all the poor ever see of the rich - those great fat overhanging arses that part every now and again to rain down their blessings. Royal shit's a miracle they say - cures fevers and the clap. Makes a lovely stew.

ALICE: I think that's quite the most horrible thing I've ever heard!

CARROLL: You just haven't lived long enough. Did I ever tell you about my schooldays?

ALICE: No, but I'm sure you fully intend to. Otherwise, why mention it at all?

CARROLL: Yes. Well.. I went to Rugby. Or rather Dodgson went to Rugby. Wishy-washy, watery-weak Dodgson. A sickly child. Pale and imaginative - target for every upper class bully boy in that charming corner of the Empire. Can you imagine it? Debagging rituals, vicious baptisms in the boys lavatories! Oh God, I can still smell the soap!

'We'll make a man of you yet, boy!' And they'd thrash with their canes!

Oh yes, the spirit that makes England great is forged on those playing fields. In a refiner's fire of humiliation and sodomy and bloody Greek grammar!
This country, this Empire, stands tall on a foundation of buggery and bullying. The happiest days of our lives!
I remember Dodgson spread-eagled across a desk. He could smell the ink in the inkwell, follow the grain of the wood. Truscott on one side, Harris on the other, holding him down. Rudman at the back. Good at games, arrogant. Officer material. I'm sure you know the type. That was Rudman. Dodgson heard him fumbling with his buttons. He smelled ink and

thought of words on parade, of all the words that ink might become.

ALICE: Didn't you.. I mean, didn't he try to struggle or fight?

CARROLL: Against what? Against a whole culture bearing down on him, stinking of yesterday's buttered muffins and honest manly sweat? How could one small boy be expected to fight against that? Anyway, it was part of growing up, part of becoming a man. The school of hard knocks. The short sharp shock. No, Dodgson just lay there and thought of England. He didn't struggle.

ALICE: And then?

CARROLL: Did I tell you about Edward the Second?

ALICE: You never quite seem to finish telling me about anything.

CARROLL: Edward of Caernarfon. King of England. 1284 to 1327. He couldn't hold the country together. Trouble with the barons. You know how it is...Eventually he was overthrown and they had him put to death in rather an interesting fashion.
They pushed a hunting horn up into his...well, his tradesman's entrance, you might say. A hunting horn!

ALICE: But the only tune that he could play was 'Over the hills and far away.'

CARROLL: Quite. Anyway, one of that rebellious crew had heated a poker in the brazier. The metal was white-hot, glowing. And there was poor Eddie, poor Ted, with his knock-knees knocking and his pipe-cleaner legs and a hunting horn sticking out his arse. Well, he was asking for it, wasn't he?

ALICE: I can't imagine.

CARROLL: Then try. Try to imagine that white hot poker rammed up the hunting horn, like a train into a tunnel. The short sharp shock!

(CARROLL's voice reaches a crescendo. He ends on a scream. Pause.)

He won't be in any hurry to rule a country again, I can tell you! They say Edward's screams were heard in the next county but they'll say anything won't they?
Anything for a laugh.

ALICE: I don't know what the point of all that was.

CARROLL: The point? Don't talk to Edward the Second about points, dear!
So where was I? Oh yes.. Dodgson, stretched across that old school desk with his trousers round his ankles and Rudman deep in the heartland. Dodgson suddenly understood why Edward the Second had screamed so loudly and why that yodelling yell had resounded down

through the pages of English history. He understood and, in that hot fire of biblical revelation, I like to think he first became aware of me.

ALICE: But what exactly did he understand?

CARROLL: That scream, that terrible cross-county scream, was a cry of pure delight!

ALICE: I don't see how you can possibly work that out. It makes no sense at all.

CARROLL: Mathematics, little Alice, mathematics. The plus and minus of existence, the algebra of the human spirit.
Edward's cry was the cry of a liberated soul. All those years as King, trying to rule with an iron hand. How he must have longed, just for once, to leave it all behind and become the lowest of the low. Legs apart like a tuppeny whore, free at last of all responsibility.
And today, nearly six hundred years later, England struts around in all its finery, with ships and crystal palaces and steam engines - ruler of the world. An Empire lies sprawled at England's feet. And yet, if England ever dared face itself in the mirror, what would England see?

ALICE: I suppose it would see 'England' backwards. Which would be..

CARROLL: *(Interrupting.)*It would see a guilty schoolboy just longing to be caught in the act by nanny! A spanking from the governess! Deep in our hearts we know that's what we need. Why else would we put up with that stern old bag Victoria?

ALICE: Lady Lyon says that a 'vein of iron' runs through the Queen.

CARROLL: The Iron Lady. Yes, I've heard it said.
In one of my stories, I wrote about the Red King, remember?

ALICE: 'Through the Looking Glass'. Chapter four.

CARROLL: That's the one. The Red King slept under a tree, dreaming away his life.
And what was his dream?

ALICE: He dreamed the world into being.

CARROLL: That's right. Everything in the world - you and me, the birds and the bees, the flowers and the spiders, the cats and the cockroaches and all the words in all the books...
All of it, is part of his dream and if he were ever to waken up, we'd all go out
BANG!

(CARROLL snaps fingers.)

ALICE: Like candles!

CARROLL: All of our lives we spend living in someone else's dream. Sometimes it's a good dream but most of the time it's bad. Right now, we're forced to inhabit the sick dream of Victoria. We're all part of it. Because of her, all this has come to be!

(Indicating East End London with a sweep of his arm.)

And we all bend over gladly for the old governess, the Iron Lady, Miss Birch, mistress of discipline!
And yet she's mad! Victoria is mad! She lives in overheated rooms. She surrounds herself with mementoes and souvenirs. No-one is allowed to knock on her door. Only a gentle scratching is permitted for fear that she might fully awake and we would all cease to exist.

ALICE: BANG!

CARROLL: Like candles. And every night at Windsor, Albert's clothes are laid out on the bed. Perhaps she hopes that her husband's spirit will come to fill the clothes. Perhaps she clambers on top of them and rubs her dry skin against the crotch of his regimental trousers, cutting herself on his medals.. The old boy's probably more fun now than he ever was when he was alive.

ALICE: I don't think I like this dream Mr. Carroll. I don't think I like this story at all.

CARROLL: It doesn't matter whether or not you like it. We're all stuck in it.

Water, too. Fresh water is placed in Albert's basin every morning. The Queen sleeps with a photograph of him over her bed. Not a photograph of him when he was alive, mind you, but a photograph of the dead Albert. Our culture is rooted in a death obsession. It's sick with repression. We've endured the longest reigning Monarch in English history. That's a long time to dream the same dream. Is it any wonder we long to awake?

You know, it always seemed highly significant to me that the Queen loved my stories. Funnily enough, after reading 'Alice's Adventures in Wonderland', the mad old hag ordered all the other works by the same author.

ALICE: I'm sure she was surprised when she received them.

CARROLL: Yes. They sent her Dodgson's dry as dust 'Condensation of Determinants' and 'Euclid and his Modern Rivals' and all those other cures for insomnia. I wish I could have seen her face!

On second thoughts, I have seen her face and once was more than enough.

ALICE: May I ask a question now?

CARROLL: If you like. And if it's a good one, you can move forward four spaces.

ALICE: Why didn't you write any new stories? It's been such a long time since 'Through the Looking Glass'. Why was I left for so long without any adventures?

CARROLL: You grew up. You crossed the line. Grown-ups don't have adventures. They have gas bills.
Dodgson tried to do something new. He's been writing and he's produced some awful thing called 'Sylvie and Bruno' which he plans to publish next year.

ALICE: I don't think I like the sound of either Sylvie or Bruno.

CARROLL: A pair of charmless upper-class brats. I'd have drowned them both at birth if it had been me. Or perhaps I'd send Bruno to Rugby. They'd make a man of him there.
Anyway, the book's horrible. He tried to do it without me. Can you imagine it? The stuttering deacon searching his fossilised mind for one original thought and finding only cobwebbed equations and creaking formulae. A wall of glass that he could no longer push his way through. Poor Dodgson. I'd feel sorry for him if I wasn't such a bastard. He thought he could get by without me! He thought he could shut me out!

ALICE: Perhaps you were beginning to outstay your welcome. Like a rude uncle at Christmastime.

CARROLL: Admittedly, my influence was getting stronger. I was beginning to make all the important decisions. I mean, it was I who encouraged him to develop his friendships with little girls. I who stimulated the creative side of his nature.

ALICE: The photography?

CARROLL: Yes. It's funny you should remember that. You always were the best, Alice. The camera seemed to bring out the savage in you. That look in your eyes went way beyond your years. The shawl slipping, just so, off your shoulders.

(ALICE strikes a sexy, smouldering pose. CARROLL mimes taking her picture.)

Click. Flash!

(She continues to strike attitudes, Vogueing shamelessly.)

All those times he dreamed of being cast up on a desert island with you.

(The light turns red.)

Together in the dark room. Dodgson's stutter was always wuh-wuh-wuh-worse.. worse in the dark room. The pictures reversing into existence in the developing fluid.
Click. Flash!
Family studies at first. Then costumes. Little girls only, of course. Dressed as savages or urchins. Dressed in rags. With that look on your face, Alice.

(ALICE smoulders at him. Her posing becomes more suggestive, more provocative.)

That's it! Yes! Those eyes!

(CARROLL becomes more excited as ALICE postures and teases.)

And when the costumes weren't enough, I whispered in his ear, 'Do it! Do it! Do it!'
Click. Flash!
Such charming studies, Mr. Dodgson. Of course, there's no harm in it. So perfectly pure and lovely.
My God, how he sweated! Perfumed children. That white skin, smooth as milk.
Click. Flash!

(CARROLL crawls towards Alice. His cane, outstretched, hovers around her thighs. He reaches forward, touches her arse, then pauses, then pulls away, overwhelmed.)

You bloody little tease.

ALICE: *(Haughty.)* I'm sure I don't know what you mean, Mr. Carroll. I thought this was all a game.

CARROLL: Well, it was. Unfortunately, the parents didn't see it in quite the same way. There were complaints. Discreet complaints, mind you. This is England, after all. Nevertheless.. friendships were terminated. Of course, Dodgson hadn't actually done anything. He only wanted to look. That was all. As for me, I.. I wanted to..

(CARROLL, almost inarticulate. Spitting fragments of sentences. Wracked with frustration.)

...wanted to.. little misses.. on the carpet.. squeal.. I'd make them. A hot knife into butter!

(He regains control.)

But Dodgson banished me. Exorcised me. Never again would he give in to his base desires. No more photography. No more Alice. No more rabbit holes and magical mirrors. No more Snarks and Boojums.

(Derisive now.)

Sylvie and Bruno. The lobotomy twins.

ALICE: Funny he never married.

CARROLL: He had his eye on you for a while, dear. In those days, the age of consent in England was 12. Dodgson, of course, always terminated his friendships when the girls reached 12. Old hags! In these more enlightened days, we've come to realise that girls of 12 simply don't have the emotional maturity to enter into sexual relationships. We've raised the limit. It's 13 now.

ALICE: My age exactly.

CARROLL: Unlucky for some. What an idiot Dodgson was. He needed me, you know? He needed me. He knew it the first time he changed his name. 1856. Oh, he realised he was onto something good. Let me tell you, when Dodgson changed his name it was an act of magic. An invocation. Charles Lutwidge Dodgson. Take away the surname and what do you have?

ALICE: Charles Lutwidge, of course.

CARROLL: Latinise it.

ALICE: That would be.. Carolus Ludovicus!

CARROLL: Flip that through a mirror to make it English again...

ALICE: Lewis Carroll!

CARROLL: Oh yes. Yours truly!
That name became a conjuration. Lewis Carroll. Lewis Carroll. The spirit of unreason, the demon of nonsense, the unbound Prometheus.

(CARROLL begins to rave with hysterical triumph. His body goes into spasms. Spastic birth trauma.)

It was like fire. Dodgson's brain on fire! Stuttering Dodgson in his study, with the words stuck like hooks in his tongue. The name. Say it! Lewis cuh-cuh-cuh-Carroll. Cuh-cuh-Carroll! He called and I replied. I rose up out of the sludge and the shadow!

(CARROLL's voice rises hysterically. He rolls into a foetal position. Bucks and kicks in the throes of transformation. Then onto his knees, clutching his head as though trying to hold it together. Agonised.)

Carroll rising like a devil in the smoke. Splitting his head like an eggshell, like an atom, like a china cup. Carroll being born, born screaming and bursting like pus from that tortured cess-cellar of a skull!

(The voice reaches a peak of frenzy. Then, he is suddenly quiet. He shoots a sidelong glance, almost of amusement.)

Are you following me so far?

ALICE: I'm not so much following as going on ahead.

(ALICE looks at him, suspicious. She runs the toe of her shoe around the chalk outline. She steps into it.)

ALICE: Mr. Carroll, do you think that if I stand in here, it will protect me? Like a magician's chalk circle?

CARROLL: Protect you? Protect you from what?

ALICE: Why, from the Minotaur. From demons of course.

CARROLL: Perhaps but only if you recognise them first. Sometimes, I think 'demon' is just another word for 'mirror'. Through a Looking Glass Darkly, if you like. I don't think we really have to look to Hell for our demons, do you? What is Hell but London's reflection in a puddle of dirty water? What is Hell but the maze that lies behind the walls of our own skulls.

ALICE: And so Alice came at last to the centre of the Labyrinth. Or have you forgotten the story?

CARROLL: Oh, that.. yes..

ALICE: And what did she find there? I don't see the Minotaur anywhere.

CARROLL: You're just not looking hard enough. In the centre of the Labyrinth, Alice found another dream. This one nested inside Victoria's dream, snug as a Russian doll. There is a Minotaur, dragging the chains of repression behind him. There is a Red King, Alice. Little Miss Hieroglyph there will tell you that. The whores of Whitechapel will tell you that.

(He begins to circle ALICE, menacing.)

Every night they walk through the dream of the Red King, wondering if tonight will be the night when they finally get to meet him in person. It's a dream of narrow streets at three in the morning. A dream of sputtering gas-lamps and footsteps on the cobbles. No-one there. No-one there but the Red King, moving through the Labyrinth.

Stay safe in your magic circle, Alice. The Red King is real. They say I am a doctor now. Ha. Ha.

Do you know me?

ALICE: You're Mr. Dodgson but you're also Mr. Carroll and if names travel in pairs they travel in packs.

CARROLL: Yes. Yes. Those names belong to me. I am also the Minotaur. The Beast in the Maze. And I am the Red King too. I want to get to work straight away, if I get the chance. And there is another name. You know it, don't you? Everyone knows it now. That name.

(CARROLL twitches, wracked, a genuine stutter now. A sense of something cracking, pushing free.)

Juh-juh-juh-juh-JACK!

(He snaps a flick knife open in front of her face. He is instantly calm, deadly cold and in control.)

Jack.

(ALICE pretends hard not to be alarmed.)

I'm down on whores. I'm down on whores and I shan't quit ripping till I do get bucked!
        (Pause.)

The first was Mary Ann Nichols, 42, also known as 'Polly'.

(ALICE joins in, her voice flat and level. A coroner's report.)

ALICE: The throat was cut, possibly with a long-bladed knife. There were bruises on the right hand side of the jaw which appear to have been caused by the pressure exerted by fingers. The abdomen had been slashed open and there were two stab wounds in the genital area.

CARROLL: Then came Annie Chapman, 45, also known as 'Dark Annie'.

ALICE: The throat had been cut with two parallel incisions. The abdomen had been completely opened and a length of intestine severed from its mesenteric attachments. The intestines were removed and pulled up over the left shoulder of the victim. The uterus, the ovaries and a portion of the bladder had been entirely removed.

CARROLL: Elizabeth Stride, 45 , known as 'Long Liz'.

ALICE: There was a long incision in the neck, which commenced on the left side 2 inches below the angle of the jaw. It neatly severed the vessels on the left side, cut the windpipe completely in two and terminated on the opposite side, 1 inch below the angle of the right jaw. In the left hand, a small packet of cachous, wrapped in tissue paper.

CARROLL: Catherine Eddowes, 43, also known as 'Kate Kelly'.

ALICE: The throat was cut across to the extent of 6 or 7 inches. The internal jugular vein was open to the extent of an inch and a half. The walls of the abdomen were laid open from the breast downwards. The liver was slit. There was a stab wound in the left groin and below that a cut of 3 inches, wounding the peritoneum.

(Pause.)

You're not a happy man, are you, Mr. Jack? What exactly are you?

CARROLL: What am I? I'm an eruption. I'm a fugitive from the right brain, the Dionysian hemisphere. I'm the reflection of the Age in which we live. It happens. It happens at the end of a century - this pent-up frustration must find some expression. So, it explodes like steam released from a kettle, like volcanic pressure. Is it any wonder people get hurt?

CARROLL: And London too! Look at London! Schizophrenic city. Divided like a brain into West End and East End. Into rich and poor. The haves and the have-nots. Look around you! Here in the East End, the tenements stand tall in the stink of their own filth. Cellars flooded with liquid sewage. Look! Women and children, asleep on bags full of straw, seething with fleas. Wallpaper hanging in infected strips. The very air we breathe is a thick brew of poison. Jesus! It smells like God and the Devil and all the angels farted in the face of the world.

On the streets, here on these very streets, mothers sell the virginity of their daughters to West End gentlemen. Eight! Seven! Six years old!

(CARROLL assumes music hall mock-Cockney accents.)

Yours for the price of a cup of tea, guv'nor! Strike a light an' blow me down! It's a proper to do an' no mistake!

(His own voice returns, level.)

And yet, not five miles from here, there is another world. Through the Looking Glass. In that city , children sleep in feather beds and play with dolls houses big enough to accommodate whole East End families. Father tinkles the ivories and mother sings, sweet as a nightingale. The legs of the piano are always covered, of course. Who knows what passions might be aroused by the sight of those shapely supports? Such good people, such kind people.

The sort of people who write letters to the 'Times', complaining about the 'scum of London.'

What do you remember about last year?

ALICE: *(Thinks. Decides.)* It was the Queen's jubilee..

CARROLL: Yes. Fifty glorious years! What else, though? What else happened last year?

ALICE: Well...Was it a Leap Year, perhaps? I've never quite understood where the extra day comes from..

CARROLL: You're so sweet, Alice. So innocent...Bloody Sunday is what I'm trying to say. November 13th, 1887. Bloody Sunday.
Picture the scene; hundreds of unemployed workers, camped out in Trafalgar Square.

(ALICE holds her nose.)

ALICE: Poo!

CARROLL: They had nowhere else to go, bless 'em. So they filled Trafalgar Square like sardines in a tin. It was a godsend to the bleeding hearts and the charitable institutions - all that mass of poor in one place. And so central too!
A newspaper report at the time called it 'a foul camp of vagrants.'
Others were not so kind.
The Metropolitan Police Commissioner was Sir Charles Warren. He tried to rid the Square of its human litter but those dirty devils would not budge. Sir Charles demanded additional powers. And got them.
Can you see it? On that cold day in winter - four thousand constables! Three hundred mounted constables! Three hundred Grenadiers! Three hundred life guards!

ALICE: *(Ecstatic.)* Yes!

CARROLL: Not to mention the seven thousand constables held in reserve in case all those starving, freezing people proved too tough to handle.

ALICE: Did they line up like chess men?

CARROLL: They did! The soldiers of light against the legions of darkness.

ALICE: Were they as brightly coloured as playing cards?

CARROLL: Brighter. All fired up with righteous anger. And the people, cheering them on against the unemployed.
How dare they starve? How dare they dress in rags? In front of us !

('Rule Britannia' begins to play. Carroll, excited, mimes the swinging of batons.)

The armies clashed! England at war with England. Fighting its own reflection like a Japanese fish. Batons and iron bars rose, fell, cracked skulls, shattered bones! Smash! Crack! Blood in the gutters!

(The music fades. The light returns to normal.)

It was a glorious victory, wasn't it?

ALICE: I don't know. I'm not quite sure I understand the rules.

CARROLL: The poor retreated - back to their own half of the board. Back to rot in their own dark hemisphere, where babies paddle in piss and gin. Out of sight, quite out of mind.
The month following, the Queen conferred upon Sir Charles Warren a Knight Commandership of the Bath.

ALICE: I expect he'll have been glad of that after all those dirty people!

CARROLL: But what did he really do? It was a temporary measure at best. He shut them in the cellar, like a crowd of dirty thoughts. He hid the mirror so that Victoria wouldn't have to look at her own corrupted face. He woke up and pretended it was all a dream. He covered the legs of the piano, shall we say?

ALICE: But what would you have done, Mr. Carroll?

CARROLL: Cut out the dead wood, I say! Off with their heads! We have to look forward to the '90's. We have to make cuts! Some may suffer, I know, but isn't that always the way? The weak go to the wall but the strong will always survive.
We must stamp on the poor now before they rise up to overwhelm us! In the Reading Room of the British Museum, right under Victoria's nose, Karl Marx wrote Das Kapital and even as we speak that unspeakable book is being read by a pale young malcontent in Kazan - Vladimir Illich

Ulyanov, who will, very shortly change his name..

God, I can almost hearing them singing now. The music of revolution. 'Then raise the scarlet standard high!..'

I'll give them scarlet!

I'll give them bloody gallons of it!

(Regains his composure. He steps back. Expression and accent softens.)

Step over your chalk lines, Alice.

ALICE: Is it safe?

CARROLL: Come on.

ALICE: But is it safe?

CARROLL: Safe as a slither down a rabbit hole. Safe as a jaunt through the mirror. Step over the line.

(ALICE steps over.)

ALICE: Well.. it's not much different outside than in.

CARROLL: It never is.

ALICE: I've reached the centre of the Labyrinth only to find that there's no-one here but you, Mr. Carroll. And I must say, you don't make a very frightening monster. I'm not sure that this will make such a good story after all.

What am I supposed to do now?

(CARROLL reaches out, mimes gripping a piece of cord and cutting it with his knife. As he talks he folds the knife up and puts it away.)

CARROLL: There. I've cut your silver thread.

ALICE: Well! That's exceedingly rude! I didn't give you by your leave to do anything of the sort. What's to happen to me now? I take it I shan't be home in time for supper.

CARROLL: You can take it if you want but please remember to bring it back again.

ALICE: I'm quite sure I don't know what you're talking about.

CARROLL: You can never leave, Alice. You're trapped forever in Dodgson's head. In my head. You can never leave but look on the bright side - you won't have to grow up or grow old or die..

ALICE: I was rather looking forward to growing up, if you don't mind.

CARROLL: It's no fun. Honestly.

ALICE: *(Miffed.)* Well then. I hope you plan to keep me amused.

(CARROLL is briefly unsure. He looks away, then turns again to ALICE. He seems to seek reassurance. To find some reason not to kill her.)

CARROLL: Yes. Well, there's one last thing.. I..

Alice, please.. dear Alice.. did you ever love me?

(Street-sounds fade up. Reality reasserting itself. Alice's posture changes. She is suddenly, aggressively interrogative. An Irish accent.)

ALICE: Well?..

(CARROLL confused, as if he's just woken up.)

CARROLL: I beg your pardon?

ALICE: I haven't got all night, sir. A girl's got to earn a living, ent she?

CARROLL: What?..

ALICE: Well, you wanted me to dress up like this. It was your idea, sure. And you haven't said a word since we got here. Now, come on! D'you want it on the bed or up against the wall? It's extra for French.

CARROLL: What's...French?

ALICE: Oo! So it actually talks! What's French? A bit of the old Napoleon. You know... here comes a chopper and that..

CARROLL: What.. what's your name?

ALICE: Alice, sir. You said. I was to call myself Alice..

CARROLL: No. No, your real name.

ALICE: It's Mary Kelly. Marie Jeanette Kelly, I mean.. if you fancy the parlez-vous..

(CARROLL begins to understand. He half-smiles.)

CARROLL: Well then, Marie. Jeanette. Kelly. We seem to have been talking at cross purposes, don't we? Yes, I think..

(He thinks, comes to a conclusion.)

..I think it would be best if you just had a lie down.

(ALICE lies on the floor, smiling.)

ALICE: Lie down? Here? Why, are you going to surprise me, sir?

CARROLL: Something like that.

ALICE: Oh, I do feel tired. I've had a hard day on me back.
Won't you join me, sir? You seem like a nice sort of gentleman.

CARROLL: I do, don't I? I seem like a nice sort of gentleman. Respectable. Educated. You'd trust me with your life.

ALICE: *(Sleepy.)* Mmmm

(Pause. CARROLL looks down at ALICE curled up. He is talking as if to himself. Light fails until only

CARROLL'S face remains like a lantern, spectral in the gloom.)

CARROLL: It's 3.30. The soul's midnight. The time when most people die. These endless hours. And this room is so hot. The walls seem to sweat with it. Outside the rain falls down through darkness. We are all falling down through darkness...

(He crouches down by ALICE. Strokes her hair. She murmurs in her sleep, shifts slightly. CARROLL's voice assumes a lullaby tone. Then, he takes a piece of chalk from his pocket and begins to outline her body as he recites.)

CARROLL: 'A boat beneath a sunny sky
　　　　　Lingering onward dreamily
　　　　　In an evening of July -

　　　　　Children three that nestle near,
　　　　　Eager eye and willing ear,
　　　　　Pleased a simple tale to hear -

　　　　　Long has paled that sunny sky:
　　　　　Echoes fade and memories die:
　　　　　Autumn frosts have slain July.

　　　　　Still she haunts me, phantomwise,
　　　　　Alice moving under skies
　　　　　Never seen by waking eyes.

　　　　　Children yet, the tale to hear,
　　　　　Eager eye and willing ear,
　　　　　Lovingly shall nestle near.

In a Wonderland they lie,
Dreaming as the days go by,
Dreaming as the summers die:

Ever drifting down the stream -
Lingering in the golden gleam -
Life what is it but a dream?

(Pause. CARROLL has taken the knife from his pocket. The light turns red. His voice rises towards a crescendo.)

CARROLL: We have drunk too much from a bottle marked 'poison'.
Alice?
Wake up, Alice.
Wake up, England.
Wake up.
(She does not stir. Sudden snap and flash of blade. Single ominous bell stroke and the stage is plunged into darkness. Pause. There is a terrifying scream. A scream of horror and pain. Carroll, screaming like a woman. Pause. Scratchy record begins to play - 'Ain't She Sweet'. The 1927 version by Gene Austin.)

'There she is, there she is
There's what keeps me up at night...'

(Song continues through darkness. Ends.)

LOVECRAFT IN HEAVEN

LOVECRAFT picking scabs from the mirror, tearing away flakes of sick skin and dried blood, to expose the glistening surface beneath. Raw and wet, the mirror reflects the face of a monster - hollow-cheeked, two-eyed, pale and bloodless. The mirror is dying.

'Cancer of the glass,' Lovecraft is told. He reaches out to touch the thing he no longer recognises as his own reflection. Long, feminine fingers pass through the glassy membrane, causing ripples and little cries.

'God in Heaven,' Lovecraft sighs. 'It's brine.'

The mirror fluxes, alive with uncanny tides and the odours of pure creation. Sweet rotten scent of biological mystery. He stares into the depths as something stirs far below, wakens and begins to rise. Storms and rain wrack the mirror's surface. The thing is coming up from the deep, getting bigger and bigger. It is vast and primitive and he knows its name.

Dying on a bed in an overheated room. The air is thick, like a glue drawn into the lungs. There is something at the back of his head, scrabbling there where there is no light: rats sharpening their claws on the wood-panelled walls of the Pilgrim Fathers, the hiss and crackle of cerebral lightning. A slow, drugged voice speaks of the Ritual of the Stifling Air as the way through.

Lovecraft whimpers, dying. His body is devouring itself. He can feel the cancer at work, the ancient crab in his gut, self-generating, self-begetting. He can smell the fish-stink of it seeping through his pores. The old starry crab there in the pit of his body.

Lovecraft's eyes roll and the room divides.

Angles collide and implode. In these last days, he often wakes from delirious sleep to glimpse the room reforming itself out of nothingness, the pieces flying together out of the void, as though magnetised, to re-assemble, like an explosion in reverse. Once, this strange reconstruction of things was done in a rapid, stealthy manner, now it occurs slowly, allowing him longer and longer periods of time in which to contemplate the Ultimate Absence upon which the world is founded.

Inside him, in the dead cell, he can feel what he knows to be words, like maggots, eating at him. Words giving birth to words and more words; all the things he dared not say. (And if words are maggots, he speculates in a clear space between gusts of pain, what do these larvae become when it is time to mature and metamorphose? What will come a-hatching from his cannibalised body?) He is becoming a thing of words, a word-crab built for descent into the dark.

His own stories have turned on him in the wet interior night, growing beyond his control. Blind restless mouths, zodiacal pincers and claws, the deep sea smell of his death, like her smell, the archaic scent of his wife, his lunatic mother in her chains. His death that he smelled in the marine chambers of her cunt so long ago and refused to recognise.

The room is alive, more alive than ever, with unearthly angles. It extends itself into unspeakable trans-Euclidean topographies, breathing and shivering, presenting the dying man with grotesque displays of architectural deformity. The room reverses through itself, defying reason. Words leak from Lovecraft's papery skin and fume in the light. The Universe is made of words, he thinks. I have built my own tomb and furnished it. He strains to understand, teetering on the edge of an ocean of limitless ink. The ink of the Void in his pen, flowing out to stain the dean world. The room remakes itself. The candle-flame by his bedside dips and flutters as the room eats oxygen and the flame is bent backwards, turning black. The wings of a moth whirr against the windowpane, like the buzzing voice of a spirit stuck in a bottle.

'The Inverse Flame is the Second Gateway,' the spirit insists. The sentence is repeated several times and then dissolves into incoherence.

'Cthulhu fhtagn. Ph'nglui mglw'nafh Cthulhu R'lyeh wgah'nagl fhtagn.'

Lovecraft shifts his head and the room lurches. He looks into the wavering door of black flame but he cannot take the step through into the Cold Wastes. He snatches another breath from the abrasive air and falls from a terrible height back into the pillow.

'All my life I have believed in the God of Reason, the Master Maker with his compass and dividers and his Plan. But the Gods are mad, blind horrors and all our lives are as the dust in their eyes.'

He dare not look through the tear he has made in the Veil. Lovecraft's breath catches at the back of his throat and turns sour there. The galleries of his brain begin to flood with endorphins in a sweet opiate rush.

Stories disintegrate and fill the room like flying ash. Ash in his head. A blizzard of atomic debris, stories tearing themselves apart, reconfiguring, creating new stories endlessly. A carrion storm of words eating him from within, descending upon him from outside. His soul, at last, faces annihilation.

Ideas condense from nuclear chaos. Lovecraft stops at the top of the hill to make some notes in his black book. He wipes his brow, inclines his head to gaze at the vibrating Providence sky and walks on. In this late afternoon light, the town seems queer and other-worldly. Rooftops proliferate and recede into smoky chiffons of drowsing air. Providence seems to slumber and breathe, its uncertain horizons giving life to ambiguous forms: melting gables and rotting bridges and half-seen windows reflecting alien suns. He imagines the town as the three-dimensional shadow of something vast and concealed and then dismisses the thought as irrational. Briefly, he studies his left hand, with its parchment-white dry skin and knotted tracery of blue submerged highways. He can feel his blood, circulating through the buried tributaries and unlit canals of his body. His fingers crab and contract into a fist, the nails nipping his palms. He makes a few more jottings in his book and continues.

Evening sun casts a slow, syrupy light on the old stones of the cemetery. Lovecraft wanders among the graves, gently strobed by leaf shadows. A light breeze, the exhalation of spirits, stirs the branches as Lovecraft walks, a living man haunting the houses of the dead. He pauses at the graves of his mother and father and stares at the earth. A bird begins to sing, then changes its mind. Silence descends like a mist.

And in that silence, he can hear the creak and splinter of buried wood. He closes his eyes. The tattered, flayed corpse of his father is clambering through the wet earth into his mother's coffin, prising the lid away with broken-stick fingers, eager for her fresher flesh. Mother, with blue-bruised skin, peels back her teeth and hisses. Father, corrupt, insane, tears through her bridal veil, puncturing her rotten flesh and mindlessly fucking the punctures. The two bodies squirm and knot in a tangle of greasy, ruined limbs. Father's swollen cock bursts and spills maggots, spits obscene crawling words. The earth goes into spasm, vomiting up the dead, exploding them into space.

The bird continues to sing, out of tune, hideous. Lovecraft chews his lip, contemplative, and takes the notebook from his pocket. He writes two words - a title - and closes the book.

That night, he dreams of the spirochetes in his father's bloodstream. He enters with them through the tiny fresh cut in his father's penis. It's some kind of reverse conception through this temporary door. It's the breakthrough into another universe. The spirochetes spin like galaxies, bursting through from outside, joyously breaching Father's outer walls. Lovecraft's final human thought is to pronounce the barbarous words which open the gate, the dream incantation which becomes meaningless to him even as he utters it.

'Treponema Pallidium.'

'I dreamed that I was a syphilis bacterium invading my own father's body,' Lovecraft tells the dark room. Shadows hang in drifts from the rafters. In the hot dark, Lovecraft guiltily masturbates, finally dribbling infected come into a soiled handkerchief.

No-one strikes him down. No God, no Satan. No Heaven, no Hell. There is no judgement. The night is empty and sweats darkness.

'TT LOOKED MORE LIKE THE FATHER THAN HE DID!'

The final breath seems to last forever. It buzzes there behind his teeth. He knows it is one of the Calls and tries not to utter it.

There is an eye in the disturbed mirror. It fills the space within the frame, protozoic, contemplating nothing but itself. The gilt frame of the mirror contracts towards a lens shape, as though it were the lids of the ophidian eye slowly closing.

Sonia's cunt dilates in the New York summer heat. The room is stifling and smells of the ocean. Lovecraft enters her convulsively, clenching back the nausea that bubbles in his throat. She loops her legs around him and lets out a long breath. She bites his ear, whispers some Slavic endearment. He does not recognise the words. He hears only the guttural grunting of something buried deep in his spine.

Atavistic sound of huddled inhuman things below disarrayed stars. The clock stops ticking and he empties his terror into her arctic gulfs, her cold wastes, her cellar spaces, going inside and out simultaneously. His prick goes soft inside her, with a great oceanic seizure and he finds himself walking along the train-tracks.

'Clearly, I was not made for marriage. Mine has been a solitary life and I find that I am best able to work under those conditions. I have, it's true, often felt a certain kinship with many of the so-called Decadent authors of the last century, although I find in their work a lamentable tendency towards superstition which I most certainly do not share.

Illness and solitude do indeed produce a heightened state of creativity but we should beware of attributing to our delirious imaginings any objective validity. Nevertheless, it has been my experience that from the rich soil of morbidity grow the most fantastic flowers of the Imagination.'

He passes the carcass of an empty carriage, rotting in the half light. Red rags are hung from the broken windows. Weeds grow between the sleepers. From inside the abandoned carriage, he can hear the sound of a woman or a man whimpering. The windows flare with a putrid light and Lovecraft catches a glimpse of some diseased, abnormal thing rearing up against the glare. The whimpering increases in volume, becoming cries of pain or ecstasy.

From out of the grainy, luminous dark of this unnatural evening come the mocking cries of whippoorwills. Psychopomps, human-headed birds, they watch from the reeds, attending Lovecraft's disintegrating soul. When he passes through the gate, they will eat what remains, digest it and release the waste into the sleeping heads of humanity. Eating souls, shitting dreams.

Lovecraft pulls up his collar, following the rails down to the gutted corpse of a fishing town. Dark empty houses lean together across wet cobbled streets. Cranky spires and steeples twist towards a black sky abandoned by stars. The windows of the houses are hidden behind worm-eaten shutters. He looks towards the gutter, where a dismal glow shines up through the bars of a storm drain. Something moves down there, casting its own foul light. All the way down the cobbled street to the sea, he can see that same light feebly shining from each drain opening. Something huge beyond imagining is alive beneath the town, beating like a heart, extending its pallid fibres up into the homes of the townsfolk to change them and make them part of its nauseous substance.

Rotten skeleton wharves tilt crazily towards the unseen sea. Lovecraft carefully picks his way across the slick, crumbling timbers and stands on the on the edge of what seems to him the primal ocean. Black elemental waters, black sky. The void is full of tides and noises and the deep-sea, primordial smell of Death. Air turns to poison vapour as the venoms of her cunt foam and roar, crashing against the rocks. He is on the perimeter of manifestation, on the turrets of the ruins overlooking the Abyss. The ghost-songs of the whippoorwills resolve into insane fluting loops of synthesised sound. He recognises, from his own descriptions, the weird piping of Nyarlathotep which is the sound of the membrane trembling in ancient Night.

Lovecraft walks to the rim of existence and faces the ocean of unbeing.

That is not dead which can eternal lie
And with strange aeons, even death may die

There is a sound and the black tides begin to recede, drawn bark by the gravity of something haunted and immense which fills the sky. The seabed is opened up to view revealing decayed timbers and the bones of shipwrecks and all the corpses of the monsters of the deep. Lovecraft's body trembles uncontrollably. What nightmares lie beneath the inscrutable waves! What awesome terrors, what unbearable sights mankind has been spared! And now Earth's oceans thunder and hiss, apocalyptic, rising up impossibly, peeling back to expose the naked planet, the abyssal depths and peaks, the colossal scale of derelict, unknown continents. At last, tainted piss runs downs Lovecraft's legs as drowned R'lyeh rears up, unveiled in many-angled glory. The world is uncovered, the seas retreat like a filthy cloth drawn aside to reveal the face of an idiot leper. World eaten by maggots, boiling and bursting like a corrupted apple in space. He is witness to the revelation of the cosmic deformity of the Earth, planet of cancerous unclean energies. In terror, he curses the Mother, curses the great dark ocean and the cuntworld that is KUTULU's kingdom. His shrieks are swallowed by the blackness and the curses curdle and clot in his throat, becoming invocations. And now, there is visible not only the physical intrusion of the unmade city, but its extension into higher spaces and latitudes.

His mother screaming mad in the Butler Hospital. Endless howl of Nyarlathotep, the Faceless One, as the Gates come crashing down. The whole world sick and insane, peopled by drooling half-wits, morons swarming witlessly like maggots dying on a corpse.

City of unknown luxuries and abominations, endlessly generating itself. He is surprised by how familiar it seems. He has dreamed it so many times, this fragment of the entirety that is KUTULU, which is planetary consciousness and the Mother of Masks.

Lovecraft scribbles through the night, possessed.
CHAPTER III- The Madness From The Sea.

The gap between eye and hand is closing. The words begin on the page, not in his mind. He is conscious of them only after he has written them. So much to write in the space of a breath. Visions of things 'miles high'. ('Miles' being the only word he knows to suggest the way in which these thought-forms extend in all directions simultaneously while occupying finite spaces on this plane.) He invents the blasphemous

Necronomicon, only partially aware of the fact that he is evoking the Book into being. He is Abdul Al Hazred, 'Slave of the Presence'. The Void flows as ink through his pen. He is unwriting the Universe. Thin and sickly, hunched over a desk, defiling white paper. The headaches, the break-downs, the terrors, the fragile child surrounded by books. Shadow of the devouring mother hovering over his sickbed.

The Soul-Eater and the Gate. The pen nib sparks and ignites the paper and he makes contact through the Door of Fevers. He sees the worms eating the world, the insects in their millions chewing their way into Reality, gross and monstrous reptilian presences tearing at the walls. Black limbic fire of prophesy. Unwitting, panic-stricken, he cracks open the doorway that leads into the labyrinth of the Forgotten Ones through the fourth level of the spine. YOG SOTHOTH, the doorway that fucks itself, the eye in the mirror of water. Racing through the linked veins and capillaries of strange tunnels. Scrawling on the ancient walls. Lovecraft divides and opens like a gate, opens like the Book, but will not let them through. He hears Mother's mad graveyard voice and stops the energy deep in his gut. The primal knot clenches inside.

The last word of the story is 'eye'. He wipes his brow and closes the notebook. And closes the doorway.

18 is the number of the Crab, the worm-eaten Corpse and the Fence which divides. It is the number of the solitary, inward-turning path. Lunar Gateway of Resurrection.

Primitive societies chose their shamans from the ranks of the sick, the deranged, the outsiders. Such people can always be recognised. Frail and disconnected, they are the tenuous physical expressions of the Portals. In this way all the Doors are in plain sight, yet hidden.

Lovecraft is ushered into the quiet, dusty study of the late Professor George Angell. The Professor nods towards a leather chair, which creaks reassuringly as Lovecraft lowers himself into it.

'"Jostled by a nautical-looking negro",' the Professor says glumly, replacing a book on his shelves. The spine reads Unaussprechlichen Kulten. 'What a way to go.'

He stands before the window, silhouetted against the dark trees and the burnt-out evening sky, and fixes his gaze upon Lovecraft. 'I am forever being visited by thin, dark young men of neurotic aspect and you, I'm afraid to say, are no exception to the rule...'

Angell's voice continues, receding into a drone. Lovecraft smells old, varnished wood. Far off shouts and the laughter of Christian boys from the calm corridors of Miskatonic University. Rational light illuminates the room. The low sun turns the study into a decanter, filled with old wine.

'So what brings you here, my boy?'

'I wrote an article entitled The Cancer Of Superstition, which you may have seen' Lovecraft begins. 'The irony of my choice of title has not entirely escaped me, of course. I am also the author of a number of modest tales of the uncanny. I believe, and I say this with some little pride, that I have produced what I can only describe as the pornography of the Coming Age. I have come here to confirm my belief that the World of Reason still holds dominion over the primeval depths of the human imagination.'

Angell sits down and lights his pipe. 'An interesting theory but quite naive, I'm afraid.'

Lovecraft swallows hard. Something catches at the back of his throat, like a moth fluttering there.

'I, myself, once held to a similar position,' the Professor continues. 'But I found to my cost that I was sadly misinformed. Reason is the flimsy mask on the face of Chaos, my boy. It works very well as a disguise but, like all disguises, it conceals the truth.'

'Then our whole world is a nightmare' Lovecraft says.

The voices from beyond the doors and windows change now and become strange, like the buzzing of unknown insects. Lovecraft shifts uncomfortably and coughs. There is a pain in the pit of his stomach. Something moves there in its tiny salt ocean.

'Only if you fear it,' the Professor says.

His eyes narrow and go out, becoming empty of humanity, like the ghost-eyes of a crab.

'Perhaps I should leave now,' Lovecraft says. The failing light turns bloody and dense and he begins to choke on it. Weird liquid forms swarm around him, becoming visible.

'There is nowhere to go until you remember,' the Professor says. 'They are not dead but only dream. You must wake them within yourself and use them to step through.' He rises and rises and his shape is all wrong. The planes of the study slip out of joint. Books scream on the shelves and tear each other apart. Trees outside the window twist into spastic shapes.

Everything is dispersing.

'Filth of her cunt ... rotten ... the world ... it's in us ... the mother ... the reptile ... godforms in the backbrain ... evolutionary ... we're afraid of them ... dragging us

down, but we must ... we must embrace them ...
integrate them ... have to integrate all levels for the next
jump ... the next ... a horror ... her cunt . syphilitic ... I
failed to understand ... the horror ... shining ... Ia ...
Cthulhu ... Mother...'

'This is Hell,' Lovecraft whispers. 'I have come to
Hell.'

Angell, star-shaped, revolving in chaos, bends over
him. 'Quite the reverse,' he says and opens Lovecraft
like a door.

A half-human boy writes in his diary of the time
ahead when he will be remade in the image of his
father. High in the barn, in the alchemical light, he
dreams of lost polar corridors into the invisible and the
breaking of alien seals in the caverns of the ocean and
wonders how he shall look when the earth is cleared off
and there are no earth beings on it.

*The last breath leaves with a sound like the ticking of a
broken clock. In Arkham, along the Miskatonic, in New York
and Paris and London and Rome and Tokyo ... breaking
through ... torn black membrane ... the nameless colour ... the
egg of unbecoming ... crowned serpent ... flowering abyss ...
unfolding lens...*

Lovecraft rises up from the depths and places his
eye to the tiny peephole which looks onto the shrunken
bottle-world that was. From the other side of the
mirror, he stares at his puppet dream-self and smiles.
Full of fear, the little puppet sees only the titan eye and
misses the grin.

DEPRAVITY

(Darkness and the sound of tom-toms. An insistent, primal beat. The lights go up on EDWARD JENSEN. On the stage, there is a drawn circle with a chair in it. Outside the circle, a triangle. VICTOR NEUBERG, in darkness, sits cross-legged in the triangle.

Tom-toms stop. Jensen, picked out by light, faces the audience.)

JENSEN: Silence is not what it was.

These moments of quiet grow fewer and fewer now. And even here, there is no real cessation of noise. If you listen closely you can hear the Old Age dying and in the sound of the trams, you can hear the thin rattle of bones.

The age of certainty and dogma is dead and all that remains are the feeble voices of spirits at a seance.

Listen! There is a new sound: the sound of machines that never sleep, the sound of great engines thundering on and on through the night. Listen and you will hear the sound of wheels turning endlessly in the dark.

Unless you're deaf.

(The light changes. We see Neuberg in the triangle, staring at the floor. Jensen becomes brisk, excited. A man propounding a pet theory.)

Oh yes. The Queen is dead, boys. The Sun that never sets is slowly sinking in the West and already we see the first glimmers of a new and dreadful dawn. Something new is coming. You can feel it in the breezes that stir the dusty leaves. You can hear its awful voice in the detonation of shells over the trenches of France.

What more proof do you need? Look around you. Our artists are unravelling the world of visual perception and remaking it upon canvasses which uncover the workings of space and time. In the hands of the Cubists, the human face is reorganised into startlingly unfamiliar planes and angles. The Futurists and Vorticists capture the movement of forms through time as well as through space, creating a picture of how God must see, if God sees at all. Our poets and our writers have begun to dissect and reconstruct language itself. And in Vienna, Doctor Freud has applied these same techniques to the human mind.

We are taking apart the world and all its old certainties, as though it were a child's jigsaw puzzle, and rearranging the component parts to make a new picture. Everywhere, we are finding keys for rooms that were once locked. Everything is new; new thoughts, new pictures, new men and women.

A New Aeon.

(He steps into the circle and looks at his hand, speculatively.)

They say that lines in the palm can foretell our future. Our own hands transmit a coded message of fine grains and cross-hatchings.

Futurity engraved there upon the skin. Were we
to gaze into the palm of this new century, what
would we see there?

And were we to conjure up the presiding
daemon of this new world what would it look
like? What would it have to say to us?

NEUBERG: Oh, get on with it!

*(Jensen, mildly flustered, straightens himself, musters
his most confident tones.)*

JENSEN: Ladies and gentlemen, if I may introduce
myself. My name is Edward Thomas Jensen and
I am a physician. I will be remembered, I hope,
as one of the first English doctors to be
influenced by the revolutionary ideas of Doctor
Freud of Vienna.

NEUBERG: Kill your father, shag your mother.

JENSEN: Well, there is a little more to it than that...

NEUBERG: (Singsong.) In an angry mood, I found old
time,
With's pentarchy of Tences.

JENSEN: The human mind is no longer the unknown
country it once seemed to be. It is, rather, a piece
of precision machinery. An enchanted loom
upon which our lives are woven. Today we are
to disassemble that machine and examine its
workings.

NEUBERG: When me he spies,
>   Away he flyes.
>   For time will stay for no man.

JENSEN: That's what we do with machines which have ceased to function efficiently. Machines which have...broken down..

NEUBERG: In vain with cries,
>   I rend the skies.
>   For pity is not common.

JENSEN: There's no magic. Just plain science - a spot of oil, shall we say, to ease the meshing of the old gears. A bit of a tinker with the works.

NEUBERG: Cold and comfortless I lie.
>   Help O help or else I die.

JENSEN: It is indeed true that minds can be smashed like porcelain but we need no longer treat those so afflicted with the traditional bromides and strong chains. The days of cold water baths and scourgings belong to our barbaric past.

NEUBERG: *(Reciting now.)* Jack and Jill went up the hill to fetch a pail of water. Jack fell down and broke his crown and Jill came tumbling after.

JENSEN: Ours is a world where the extraordinary is made commonplace. Medical science has shown that the fractured mind is no longer beyond repair. We have the scissors, we have the glue and we have the will to succeed.

NEUBERG: Up Jack got and home did trot as fast as he could caper. To old Dame Dob who patched his nob with vinegar and brown paper.

(He stops abruptly.)

Poor Tom's a cold.

JENSEN: Victor Neuberg, ladies and gentleman. Victor. Benjamin. Neuberg. Neuberg, the poet.

NEUBERG: 'But the other voice was silent and the noise of waters swept me
Back into the world, and I lay asleep on a hillside
Bearing for evermore the heart of a goddess,
And the brain of a man, and the wings of the morning
Clipped by the shears of the silence; so must I wander lonely,
Nor know of the light till I enter into the darkness.'

JENSEN: Very good. 'Clipped by the shears of the silence.' Very good indeed. He works, however, in a Romantic tradition which has come to look increasingly archaic in the light of the work of Mr. Eliot and others of the Modernist tendency. A style, it must be pointed out, very like that of his late mentor and guru, Aleister Crowley. *(Pronounces it 'Croully'.)*

NEUBERG: It's 'Crow-ley'.

'It is pronounced Crowley, to remind you that I'm holy. But my enemies say Croully, in wish to treat me foully,' he used to say.
Am I friend or enemy? I cannot say.

JENSEN: You were his disciple. You suffered at his hands.

(While Neuberg talks, the doctor, becomes still. From out of the shadows, ALEISTER CROWLEY appears. Supreme confidence, dressed in dandyish style. He immediately assumes command and dominates the stage by the overwhelming potency of his presence. Poor Neuberg continues his nervous rant.)

NEUBERG: You knew him, doctor. I needn't describe him to you. Didn't you even edit some of his writings? I do seem to remember...

CROWLEY: NEUBERG!

(The voice is thunderous and unexpected. Neuberg jumps.)

What on earth are you doing? Who are you talking to?

(Neuberg looks around frantically. Caught out.)

NEUBERG: Talking? I'm not sure. I think the doctor...was...was I talking?

CROWLEY: Talking scarcely describes the hideous racket you were making. You were gibbering in a voice fit to wake the dead. In fact some of them have already lodged letters of complaint with the local magistrate.

NEUBERG: Forgive me, Guru, I was distracted by my meditations. I'd risen on the planes and resumed my vision of the temple. The one I told you about.

(He's panicky, eager to please, talking too quickly. Crowley prowls around menacingly.)

This time a maiden appeared before me. Very beautiful. Her skin had what I can only describe as a mineral quality. Illuminated from within like the interior light of a precious stone. I lay down on an altar and she took a knife and opened my breast with it. I felt the blood bubbling out, the heat of it sluicing down across my chest. I knew I was dead but the maiden began to speak and her words returned me to life.

CROWLEY: Were these four letter words?

NEUBERG: No. No! I was dead and I was restored to life!

CROWLEY: Really? I've given suits to jumble sales which had more life in them than you do, Neuberg. What happened next on this wonderful adventure?

NEUBERG: The journey continued until I came to a stream where I was tempted by a little black boy.

Then a fair woman approached me and offered herself to me. I'm proud to say I succumbed to the temptations of neither.

CROWLEY: How unadventurous of you.

NEUBERG: And then I found myself in a strange room. It smelled of old wood and polish. The light was dim, shot through with dust. Sunlight like smoke in the darkness. Someone was talking to me. A doctor with the head of an animal or bird. His shoes creaked on the floorboards, like a sign swinging in the wind. In his hands he carried a balance. I can't remember what he was trying to say. I can't remember.

(Looks up hopefully.)

CROWLEY: It's just as well you don't remember. My boredom threshold was reached and surpassed somewhere during your third sentence.

NEUBERG: I don't understand. Have I done something wrong?

CROWLEY: *(Mocking.)* 'Have I done something wrong?' You've spent the entire evening, it seems, sporting with the Qlipoth. I take it you do know what the Qlipoth are? You've wasted enough time in their loathsome company.

NEUBERG: *(Chastened. reciting.)* The Qlipoth are the negative aspects of the Sephira of the Tree of Life.

CROWLEY: Exactly. The sludge and sewage of the human mind, given form. You might as well have spent the night hanging around the public toilets of Inverness. God knows, at least you'd have picked up *something*.

NEUBERG: I didn't realise.

CROWLEY: That much is horribly obvious. It seems to me that you have deliberately squandered a valuable night's meditation. I thought I saw some potential in you, Neuberg. I thought that you had the makings of an Adept but it's clear that your aspirations rise no higher than the lowest depths of the etheric slums. I'm surprised I ever expected more from a cringing jewboy.

NEUBERG: I beg your pardon?

CROWLEY: Begging, it occurs to me, is all that you and the rest of your mongrel race are good for. Do they hand you an alms bowl directly upon snipping away your foreskin? Hmm? In fact, I would take it a stage further and suggest that the Jew has been persecuted so relentlessly that his survival has depended entirely upon the development of his worst qualities. Avarice, servility, falseness, cunning etcetera, etcetera. I'm sure you're familiar with those qualities. The shaving mirror must display them to you daily in their most degraded form.

NEUBERG: This is entirely unnecessary!

CROWLEY: On the contrary; I think it needs to be said that I have treated you, mistakenly it seems, as a human being. I realise now that you are little more than a brute representative of a brute race who understands only the wisdom of the lash.

NEUBERG: Now wait a moment! Only a cad of the lowest type would so brutally insult a man on account of his race.

CROWLEY: A cad! I may be a cad but at least I can say that I am not of a people whose closest affiliation seems to be with the most debased class of vermin. How many sewer rats did your mother have to consort with to produce you? Jew boy! Jew boy! Navy blue!

NEUBERG: I will not have my family and my race insulted in this manner.

CROWLEY: Ha'penny chew.

NEUBERG: That's quite enough.

CROWLEY: Four by two.

NEUBERG: That's enough, I said!

CROWLEY: Regent's Park Zoo.

NEUBERG: Enough!

CROWLEY: Hullabaloo.

NEUBERG: STOP IT, DAMN YOU!
(Neuberg is flushed and agitated. Pause.)

CROWLEY: Oh, for God's sake, Neuberg, you're completely hysterical. You see now what happens when you paddle in the sewers of the Qlipoth? Look at yourself. A victim of those meaningless, jabbering voices that fill the night with their incessant babble.

NEUBERG: There's no need.

CROWLEY: Their influence has made you forget that diamond strength of will which is the true magus' only shield and armour. Your armour, as I have demonstrated, offers all the protection of a yard of gauze.

NEUBERG: There's no need for such cruelty.

CROWLEY: I'll be the judge of that. If necessary, I will show you cruelty of a sort that will make de Sade look like a zealous scoutmaster. In the meantime, I've brought something for you. I know how you love flowers.

NEUBERG: Those are nettles.

CROWLEY: You have the keen eye of an expert botanist, Neuberg. Raise the hem of your robe and bend over.

NEUBERG: What?

CROWLEY: I can scarcely believe that you're as hard of hearing as you are ignorant.

(Neuberg mimes lifting a robe, kneels down and bends over.)

Perhaps this will help concentrate those wandering thoughts. Now, Neuberg. Do you deny the Qlipoth? Do you seek only the Knowledge and Conversation of your Holy Guardian Angel? Is your will an arrow that flies unerringly towards its target?

NEUBERG: Yes! YES! For God's sake!

(Before he can strike, Crowley returns to the shadows. The doctor comes forward.)

Yes.

JENSEN: Victor?

NEUBERG: I said 'yes'. Crowley beat me on a number of occasions.

JENSEN: About the buttocks? With stinging nettles?

NEUBERG: Yes. I must admit I began to suspect that he was a homosexual sadist.

JENSEN: A shrewd deduction, I must say. But what about you? How did you react to this punishment?

NEUBERG: I laughed usually. I just laughed.

JENSEN: Am I to assume that you enjoyed these lashings?

NEUBERG: I didn't mind the physical pain. It was the verbal cruelty I couldn't stand. The vicious anti-Semitism of the man. I tell you, if I hadn't taken a Vow, I'd have left his house that very day.

JENSEN: But you stayed.

NEUBERG: I waited out the entire ten day period of my magical retirement. You must understand that Crowley had shown me things that I had scarcely believed could exist. Things within myself. Things outwith me. The world we know is little more than a ghost of that greater world, doctor. We are, indeed, in Plato's cave, watching shadows on the walls. Reality is at our back.

JENSEN: Rather like Crowley, one cannot help but think. Is that all?

NEUBERG: I respected him. As a teacher. As a guru.

JENSEN: As a chap who liked to thrash other chaps' buttocks with stinging nettles?

NEUBERG: He was more than that. He was the most brilliant man I had ever encountered. I think I was in love with him. In a way. In more than one way.

(Pause.)

On the eighth day of the retirement, I entered the period of what Crowley called 'spiritual dryness'. The dark night of the soul. How can I explain that dreadful time? When all hope withers on the vine and all our aspirations seem like dust thrown into the void. It was my first glimpse of the great wheel of existence, endlessly turning. A millwheel grinding time and the lives of men and women. The Hindus know it as the Great Wheel of Samsara, which turns ceaselessly through three states of being - things rise up from darkness and inertia and are stirred into brilliant and energetic movement. The reward of this movement is a state of calmness and balance which returns again to the torpor of the original state, around and around, without rest. It's also the Tibetan Wheel of Life and the Tarot Wheel of Fortune which Jupiter spins. Keh-har, the Twentieth Aethyr.

Crowley saw in my melancholy a foreshadowing of my initiation as an Exempt Adept. A magician, freed at last from the karmic wheel of birth and death.

He was wrong. There are those of us who never escape. There are those of us who remain pinned to the Wheel.

JENSEN: What are you afraid of? I saw a shadow cross your face.

NEUBERG: Nothing.

(He listens.)

Cartwheels on the cobbles.

JENSEN: Was that the end of your initiatory period?

NEUBERG: Technically, yes. Ten days. That was to have been the end of it.

CROWLEY: The end of what? You really must try to avoid talking to yourself with such unashamed enthusiasm.

(Neuberg turns to look at Crowley.)

NEUBERG: You talk to yourself. I've heard you.

CROWLEY: Indeed. But I talk to myself simply because it's the only opportunity I'm given to indulge in intelligent conversation.
You were saying?

NEUBERG: The end of my retirement. You did say that I was to spend ten days here at Boleskine. Surely I've been fairly successful.

CROWLEY: That's for me to say.
These ten days have served purely and simply as an overture. The visions you have experienced are little more than magic lantern shows. The real work of the magus has yet to begin. Do you think you have the strength of will to continue?

NEUBERG: Yes. Yes, I think I do, as a matter of fact.

CROWELY: That's the spirit! Then you can hardly object to my wanting to put that strength to the test, can you? Here, I've prepared a bed for you.

(Crowley points at the floor. Neuberg laughs manically.)

NEUBERG: Those are gorse bushes.

CROWLEY: Once again, you astound me. It's obvious you've spent a great deal of time rambling through the woods and hedgerows with some rampantly rustic relative.

NEUBERG: You surely can't expect me to sleep there.

CROWLEY: I expect great things of you, Neuberg. Try not to disappoint me at this early stage.

(Neuberg, shocked, crouches down.)

Naked, if you please.

(Neuberg lies on the floor, gingerly. He is trying not to show pain and discomfort.)

That's it. I won't kiss you goodnight but I will wish you sweet dreams. Goodnight, sweet prince. Try not to take too much notice of the pricks.
(Crowley pauses, amused.)

That's a motto from which I've taken great
spiritual comfort in my time.

(Jensen crouches down by Neuberg.)

JENSEN: He made you lie naked on this bed?

NEUBERG: Ten nights. The cold was atrocious and my
skin was torn mercilessly by the gorse needles.
Sometimes I think that was what brought on my
tuberculosis. The hideous cold of that dreadful
room.

JENSEN: And yet still you obeyed him.

NEUBERG: He promised a new world. A world beyond
the dull round of human activity and pointless
endeavour. I had already glimpsed planes and
spheres above our own gross universe. Crowley
promised that I would learn to travel through
time and space and gain knowledge of past lives.
He promised the Knowledge and Conversation
of my Holy Guardian Angel, mastery of life and
finally the ultimate apotheosis - a rise above the
duality of the Universe. Union with the
Godhead.

JENSEN: You're lying on a bed of gorse in a damp room
in a house near Inverness and you can talk about
Union with the Godhead?

NEUBERG: *(Fiercely.)* Yes!
(Less certain now.) Ultimately, yes.

If we cannot control the body, how are we to possibly control the mind? These ordeals focus the will. The mind masters the body. Christ, it's cold. Why is he so cruel? He didn't seem cruel when I first met him. In my rooms at Cambridge. The smell of books and undisturbed dust. God, it seems like years and another world. Such a mess. Butter stains on the blotter. A fire crackling in the grate. I can see myself there. Look! I hardly recognise me. Stooped and dishevelled. Like an unmade bed. Papers scattered everywhere. Scribbled poetry. See here!

(Neuberg gets up, mimes a frantic tidying operation. Crowley reappears. He looks around, evidently amused and appalled by the disarray of Neuberg's environment.)

CROWLEY: I hope my visit hasn't inconvenienced you. Captain Fuller suggested that I drop by.

(Neuberg is very agitated and excited. Clumsy. He smoothes his clothes, his hair. Restlessly fidgeting and eager to please.)

NEUBERG: Not at all. It was very kind of you to call. I've admired your work for quite some time. One of England's finest poets.

CROWLEY: One of England's finest poets! Are you trying to tell me there is another?

NEUBERG: Sorry?

CROWLEY: We mustn't forget Mr. Shakespeare, I suppose. I imagine he is likely to be my only rival for posterity.

NEUBERG: *(Laughs nervously.)* Yes, well...I must show you some of my own poetry. It scarcely reaches the sublime heights of beauty which I find in your work but I feel that I may have some small talent.

CROWLEY: I have no interest in small talents! Think of Shelley, spirit of revolution. His eyes eaten by fish, his voice a thunder that resounds down the years and heralds the coming storm. Think of Coleridge, voyaging into the lamp-lit magical night of the opium trance, to bring back his jewelled and fantastic verses. Think of Milton. Blake. Byron. Think of Swinburne. Think above all of Crowley, who has surpassed all of these. Poetry is not a discipline for those of faint heart and small talent.

(Neuberg looks suitably awed and contrite.)

I see you wear the green star of Esperanto on your breast.

NEUBERG: Yes. Yes. I see it as a symbol of the day when all men will join hands as brothers. A symbol of the day when Babel is rebuilt in defiance of God and all men speak the same tongue. The voice of Freedom heard once more!

CROWLEY: And are you yourself fluent in Esperanto?

NEUBERG: Well, no...as a matter of fact, I'm not. I haven't managed to get around to learning the language yet.
I rather liked the badge, that's all.

(Laughs hysterically.)

CROWLEY: Quite.
It's clear, judging by the contents of your library that you have some interest in, shall we say, matters of a spiritual inclination.

NEUBERG: Yes. I have dabbled in those waters. You might even say I've caught a few fish in my time. I've had some success in the area of clairvoyance and even more so with the world of discarnate spirits. Sitting at circular tables in darkened rooms. The spit of wax candles. The whispering of gas lamps turned low.
'Is there anybody there?'

(Pause.)

'Is there anybody there?'
And the table would begin to shift. Wood creaking in protest. The shimmer and ring of ghostly tambourines. The note of a trumpet held in unseen hands. And the presences! My God! Faces like chalk drawings smeared across the dark, announcing themselves in fantastic languages. Tongues long since lost to man. Words unknown except to future time.

(Neuberg seems to enter a trance, twitching and spitting out barbaric unformed sounds.)

Guh-rakkchh shashakkkrr innainna trruchh-utt ummbruttullshhhkk-kk-rrr ow ow owkrrriiitt-tt-urrrr akkakakakaAAAAAAAAAul

(He stops and looks at Crowley for approval, pleased with his own performance.)

CROWLEY: You certainly have a way with words, Neuberg.

(Neuberg laughs again. Crowley looks at him with a kind of pity.)

Yes, indeed. You have some talent, it's plain to see. You also smell like a midden and look like a tinker who has abandoned all dignity and aesthetic criteria.

NEUBERG: I'm sorry. I think of little but my poetry and I'm afraid I've allowed my physical appearance to deteriorate somewhat.

CROWLEY: Bohemianism is all very well if one has the fashion sense to go with it. You, unfortunately, appear to have no sense of any kind whatsoever. What are we to do with you?

NEUBERG: Anything.

CROWLEY: That, it strikes me, has been your misfortune. You've allowed yourself to be the plaything of the entire spirit world.

I, however, shall teach you how to protect your aura and lead you away from the vulgar playground of spiritism. If you have the courage and the perseverance, I shall instruct you in the ways of the magus. I shall plunge you into such a fire that the purity of it shall burn up that earthly shell and elevate you into the company of angels.

Do what thou wilt shall be the whole of the Law!

NEUBERG: Yes!

CROWLEY: But first I suggest a bath. Perhaps several baths. And straighten that spine, Neuberg!

NEUBERG: It's true he cured my physical defects - a rather embarrassing varicocele. The pyorrhoea.

CROWLEY: His gums were rancid and he could paralyse a horse at a hundred paces. If I hadn't advised him to visit a dentist, he'd have lost every tooth in his head. Not to mention every friend he ever had. When God made Victor Neuberg, he quite sensibly and deliberately broke the mould and hid the pieces. I, being greater by far than God, took Neuberg apart and rebuilt him. Ecce homo! Pity about the spine.

JENSEN: Perhaps you ought to lie down if it's troubling you.

(Neuberg lies down, assuming again his position on the bed of gorse. Returning in time to that terrible night.)

NEUBERG: Yes. Yes . Curvature of the spine, you see. Incurable. Sometimes it feels as though I've been given the wrong skeleton. The skeleton of a much larger man, bent into this skin. Twisted coat-hangers jangling inside. Deformity's good for a poet, they say. Byron dragged his club foot behind him, like Satan's hoof. I don't think there's any way I can possibly straighten myself now. Not even on the racks of the Inquisition. Perhaps a nice firm mattress would help.

(He squirms, suffering on his bed, wracked with feverish thoughts.)

Oh God! The earth opens, poor Victor is drawn into the damp, open mouth of the grave. Choked with roots and multiplying worms. I become a maggot cathedral. Tiny architects at work in my flesh, unmaking my being.
Ten days on this bloody gorse. I haven't slept. Written upon by a thousand tiny quills. My skin is a palimpsest, written on over and over again until the original meaning is lost. Victor Neuberg lost forever. Skin like a parchment. These agonising hieroglyphics. I don't know who or what I am anymore!
Let me off this cruel bed!
Someone! Please!
Let me off!

(Jensen helps Neuberg to his chair.)

JENSEN: Victor. Victor! It's all right. You're here with me. Quite safe.

(Neuberg seem briefly delirious.)

NEUBERG: Is it hot in here?

JENSEN: I can open a window if you like.

NEUBERG: Hot dry breath. I feel scorched. Sky like blue glass heated in a kiln. The metal dry sun of the desert. The horizon encircles me. I am the dead centre of nothing and nowhere. A target.

JENSEN: You're in London, Victor. It's raining outside. London, remember?

NEUBERG: I remember too much.

JENSEN: Why are you afraid of circles? This constant talk of circles and wheels strikes me as evidence of some buried anxiety. What happened to you? This terrible breakdown must have its roots in some ghastly experience. What does the circle mean to you?

NEUBERG: It's nothing. Rattle of cartwheels in the rain. Did I tell you I've sometimes felt myself to be St. Catherine? Her poor body smashed on the wheel. All of us smashed on the wheel. Limbs broken by careless hands. Shattered on the spokes of the brute wheel.

JENSEN: I see.

NEUBERG: I don't think you do, doctor. I hope for your sake that you never see what I have seen.

JENSEN: No. It is essential that I see. How am I to help you otherwise?

(Jensen thinks for a moment.)

Are you familiar with the techniques of mesmerism, Victor?

NEUBERG: My whole life has been a demonstration of how one will can be moulded like clay by another.

JENSEN: I don't want to mould you. I want to help you.

NEUBERG: That's what they all say.

JENSEN: I propose that you allow me to mesmerise you and together we will dig into that skull of yours. We'll see what we can unearth down there.

NEUBERG: Like maggots, you mean? You and I burrowing in the stifling dark of my dead soul. My back hurts. This chair has grown thorns.

JENSEN: Your side of the story should be heard, Victor. You deserve the right to state your case.

NEUBERG: My testament? The Gospel according to Judas? Crowley has mastered history. The New Aeon belongs to him. What am I but a footnote in his hagiography? My words become Apocrypha. Heretical texts to inspire apostate sects.

JENSEN: I can tell you were a poet, my boy!

NEUBERG: Even my poetry belongs to the age that is gone. The modernists have supplanted me. I am buried beneath an avalanche of new words for a new world.

JENSEN: Victor, I insist that you permit me to mesmerise you. We must reach the root of this terrible pain. You cannot continue in this fashion. The Romantic Age is gone. The shadows in the asphodel woods have been dispelled by the harsh lights of a new world. I refuse to watch another young man travel down the path of melancholy and madness in the name of Romanticism.

NEUBERG: Then take care, doctor. You're opening a door that may lead to somewhere you do not care to visit. The harsh lights of your new world still cast shadows of their own.
Oh, doctor, believe me - there is a wheel that turns and never stops. They lie to us and tell us that society is 'progressing'. From hairy brutes in caves to water wheels and then to steam engines and electric power stations. Onwards and upwards, rising towards heaven, like an arrow aimed at the sun. Perfect man in a perfected world. It's all lies! There is no proud and thrusting trajectory towards paradise. There is

only the relentless turning of the wheel. We are promised the riches of the millennium and are rewarded only with the horror of ceaseless repetition. The wheel turns. Utopia is an empty confection dangled before our eyes. A tawdry bauble that catches the light.

(Jensen holds up some sparkling trinket, turning it.)

JENSEN: Like this?

NEUBERG: The Golden Dawn. The Silver Star. Charming names to mask the truth of soiled sheets and bestial couplings. Always darkest before the dawn, they tell us, forgetting to mention that the dawn is followed once more by terrible night. The promised Golden Age is so much dross. There is only one great secret and it is hidden in plain sight, doctor.

(He finishes, emphatically.)

The wheel never stops turning.

(Jensen's voice becomes even and hypnotic.)

JENSEN: Turning, Victor. Yes. The wheel turning. See the glitter of light in the spokes of the wheel.

NEUBERG: What light is that? The promised light of revelation.

JENSEN: Turning. The light turning.

NEUBERG: All that glisters is not gold.

JENSEN: You are sinking into the light, Victor. Listen to my voice, only to my voice. It buoys you up. An ocean of warm gold and you are sinking. Fathoms down into the endless light. Listen to my voice. You are safe and you are asleep. Afloat in the golden light.
Can you hear me, Victor? Listen only to my voice. Can you hear me?

NEUBERG: Yes.

JENSEN: You are quite safe, Victor. You are safe and you will obey the sound of my voice only. Your right arm has become weightless, like a balloon filled with helium. Gravity cannot hold it down. Can you feel it rising, Victor?

(Neuberg's arm rises of its own accord.)

NEUBERG: Yes.

JENSEN: Let it fall again.

(The arm goes down slowly, as in a dream.)

JENSEN: Tell me about Aleister Crowley. What made you leave him? Where are you, Victor?

NEUBERG: Paris. We're in Paris. It's January and the air is like knives. A bitter wind across the Seine. Ice floats on the surface of the river. The gargoyles roost on Notre Dame. Light trapped in the great wheel of the rose window. Crowley has no money. Neither of us has any money and he plans to invoke the gods Mercury and Jupiter in a series of devotions. These gods govern the sphere of wealth and it seemed that they might be able to help us.

JENSEN: How are the gods invoked?

NEUBERG: With sexual rites. We are like Rimbaud and Verlaine...Nothing less than the systematic derangement of the senses...Drugs, magic, a delirious intoxicating whirl of sensation. A frenzy, a bacchanal to draw down the gods. We're afraid of nothing.

(Pause.)

Crowley is afraid of nothing.

JENSEN: And what about you? What are you afraid of?

NEUBERG: I'm afraid of Crowley.

(He begins to perform a banishing ritual - a charm against possession and fear.)

I.N.R.I.
Yod, Nun, Resh, Yod.
Virgo, Isis, Mighty Mother.
Scorpio, Apophis, Destroyer.
Sol, Osiris, Slain and Risen.
Isis, Apophis, Osiris, Ee-ah-oh..

(Neuberg raises his arms in crucifixion attitude.)

The Sign of Osiris Slain.
(Right arm raised at the elbow. Left arm pointing downwards at the elbow. A swastika.)

The Sign of the Mourning of Isis.

(Raises arms in a 'V' shape.)

The Sign of Apophis and Typhon.

(Arms crossed over the breast, like a mummified body.)

The Sign of Osiris Risen.

L.V.X. Lux, the Light of the Cross.

(Jensen turns to the audience, scholarly now, as though addressing his learned friends.)

JENSEN: The Egyptian story of the murder of Osiris:
Osiris was a good and wise ruler but his brother Set was jealous of his great popularity. He tricked Osiris into a wooden chest and cast the chest into the sea. The goddess Isis, wife of Osiris, went in search of her husband's body and brought it back to Egypt where she hid it.
Set, however, found the body and cut it into fourteen pieces. These he scattered throughout the length and breadth of Egypt. Isis collected the pieces and by her arts restored Osiris to life. This became the master myth of the Aeon that bears Osiris' name. The Aeon of the God who

dies and is resurrected to life, bearing special gifts or knowledge. Osiris, Attis, Odin, Christ.

NEUBERG: *(Panicky.)* Christ above me ! Christ below me! Christ at my left side! Christ at my right side! Christ before me! Christ behind me!

CROWLEY: Christ almighty!

(He looks at Jensen.)

And don't think I can't see you. What are you? Some miserable unquiet spirit, I shouldn't wonder. Some minor demon with time on his hands? Watch if you like. It's cheaper than a 'What the Butler Saw' on Blackpool promenade.
I set myself to scourging the boy's buttocks once more. Well, someone had to do it. By this time they looked like a pair of cheese graters. I then took a razor and cut a cross into the flesh of his breast and finally bound a chain tightly around his head. It was for his own good, believe me.

JENSEN: What was the meaning of these acts?

CROWLEY: We concluded the evening with what I must delicately describe as an unnatural vice. To be honest, I find that all vices come equally naturally to me but in these matters it seems we must adhere to the gutter slang of the courts.

CROWLEY/NEUBERG: Jungitur in vati vates, rex inclyte rhabdou
Hermes tu venias, verba nefanda ferens!

JENSEN: Am I to conclude that an act of buggery took place?

NEUBERG: Oh yes. And I was that bugger, doctor. Did you know that the letters of the name Neuberg can be rearranged to form the mystic word 'Bugeren'? Strange but true.

JENSEN: The violation of social and sexual taboos can lead to a liberation of psychic energy. A damburst of repressed material. It makes its own sense.

NEUBERG: The working is successful despite my apparent impotence. According to Crowley, Mercury was in a mischievous mood and made me over-excited.

JENSEN: And was that the case?

NEUBERG: Not really. It's Crowley. I...I don't find him particularly attractive, to be honest. Platonically perhaps but not physically. It's like mounting a cheese. I don't know what I expected. Some pure and exalted Uranian love, such as Wilde spoke of in the dock.
Nevertheless, I am possessed by the god and Crowley sees the room filled with snake-wreathed staffs.
The third working results in a dual possession. Something takes hold of me and then an evil spirit manifests itself. Posing as Mercury, it enters Crowley's body.

JENSEN: You were both possessed?

(Crowley and acolytes, one male, one female, mime a series of sexual couplings and triplings.)

CROWLEY: At various times, Neuberg and I were possessed by a number of different entities. Neuberg, upon occasion, gave voice to prophecies which were later proved to be entirely untrue and ridiculous.

(Neuberg faces the audience and begins to speak, entranced. Crowley and his acolytes continue their lewd miming.)

NEUBERG: I will be married in June. It will be a lovely white wedding and the sun will shine and the bluebirds will sing their favourite song on this, my lovely day. And everyone will live happily ever after.

CROWLEY: I am the God Mercury. Messenger God. Christ-Hermes in winged sandals. I have come here now to reveal to you the supreme act of sexual magic. By this operation and by these acts of devotion, you will come to understand the workings of the Universe.
First, find a young girl. She is to be raped and then murdered.

(Neuberg takes over again as Crowley demonstrates the sexual murder of the girl, using the body of the female acolyte.)

NEUBERG: Beware, for those who adopt this rite will either succeed completely or fail utterly. There is no middle path for it is impossible to escape the ring of Divine Karma created. A great magical force is here released.

CROWLEY: The body of the girl is to be dissected into nine pieces, each of which you must offer as sacrifices to the undying gods. The head shall be given to Juno, the right shoulder to Jupiter.

NEUBERG: There will be complications of an international nature.

CROWLEY: The left shoulder to Saturn. The right buttock to Mars.

NEUBERG: These are to be feared.

CROWLEY: The left buttock to Venus.

NEUBERG: The earth will shake.

CROWLEY: Arms to Priapus.

NEUBERG: God of Panic walks the earth.

CROWLEY: Legs to Pan!

NEUBERG: Pan!

CROWLEY: Pan!

BOTH: *(Triumphant, ecstatic.)* EE-AH-OH PAN!

(Jensen, as Jupiter, showers Crowley and Neuberg with gold and silver circles of foil, representing glittering riches.)

JENSEN: A success, then?

NEUBERG: The Paris Workings were a complete success but I was left exhausted and sickened. I could go no further along the path. I set out in search of realms of shining light. Airs alive with the glittering codes of raw intelligence. Instead, I found the splintered floorboards of a Paris boarding house and the spotty buttocks of Aleister Crowley.

(Neuberg hops up, crouching in his chair. Fingers make horns.)

I dreamed of becoming an exalted magus but instead he made a goat of me. Depravity, doctor, is the state of moral corruption and I had become the head of that state. In my search for spiritual transcendence, I had found only the lowest depravity. I was led by the false light of a will o' the wisp and found myself knee-deep in a swamp of iniquity. Choronzon spoke the truth.

JENSEN: Who? What was that name?

(Neuberg becomes agitated.)

NEUBERG: Nothing. No thing. No name. That door must stay closed. Hold it closed! Hammer and nails, if necessary.

JENSEN: Calm down, Victor. You're quite safe. Did you really kill a young girl, as the spirit instructed?

NEUBERG: Both Crowley and I realised that the spirit's words smacked of black magic. We disregarded them. Crowley claimed that he would have no dealings with black magic, which is essentially an earthbound, materialistic art. As was often the case, his words and his actions failed to correspond.

JENSEN: In what way?

NEUBERG: He was not averse to murder. He murdered Ione de Forest. You remember her? The dancer. She took part in the Rites of Eleusis and became my mistress for a short time. Crowley accused her of being a Circe - sent to bewitch me from the magical path. He was furious when we began seeing each other. And then he killed her.

JENSEN: I heard that she shot herself.

NEUBERG: Only after Crowley had drawn the sign of Saturn on the door of her room. Only then.
I had to get away. In his company I had been right down in the deeps of horror, and upon the heights. I went to him and I told him I would have nothing more to do with him.

CROWLEY: Traitor! Treacherous coward! I curse you as Cain was cursed! As Judas was cursed! Men and beasts will shun you and despise you! You will

live in misery and you will die a traitor's death, hounded to the grave. And even there, there shall be no rest!
SO MOTE IT BE!

(Neuberg spasms, doubles over, falls. An agony of the spirit as well as of the body.)

NEUBERG: Things fall apart. I am smashed on the wheel. Broken into fragments. I search everywhere for the lost parts of myself. I gather them in a basket, but I can't seem to find the pieces that made me what I was.
Help me!

(Jensen cradles the twitching body of Neuberg.)

JENSEN: Victor, nothing is lost forever. Nothing is truly destroyed. Think of that.

NEUBERG: I can't think. Ideas and concepts elude me. I can no longer write. He has taken even my poetry. Words scatter like birds in flight. Babel is thrown down. Nothing has meaning. I might as well be transcribing the brute gruntings of Neanderthal man. What remains of us when even our words die on our lips, doctor? Thick dust on the tongue. The haunted inkwell thronged with the ghosts of words unsaid. Writing becomes archaeology. Digging in the ruins for fragments of something long dead. Crowley cursed me and my soul died. If only I were Judas, I would have the courage to hang myself.

JENSEN: Instead, you have come to me. Your soul's not dead but broken. Think of me as Isis, Victor. I'll gather up those scattered parts of you. I'll put them together again. A resurrection into light.

NEUBERG: Osiris? Perhaps it's right that I should identify myself with a God whose time has come and gone. You cannot bring me back to life, doctor. The best you can hope for is to raise a ghost that looks and talks like me. This isn't psychiatry, this is table-rapping.

JENSEN: You are flesh and blood, Victor. A living man who deserves to take pleasure in his life.

NEUBERG: Then why am I in the land of the Dead? Everything here is dead. The soul of things has departed. Even the chair has lost its chairness. The lamp its lampness. All the gods are dead.

JENSEN: How can you say these things? With Crowley, you helped restore those gods to life during the Rites of Eleusis. I was there! I took part.

NEUBERG: I remember. Of course, I remember. And you must know that we restored those gods only so that Crowley could slay them again and take their place.
The plot of the drama was simple: Man, unable to solve the riddle of Existence, takes counsel of the gods, one by one. None can help him. In the end, Pan appears and offers up the one true hope of the future - the Crowned and

Conquering Child of Crowleyanity. We killed the gods and set Crowley up in their stead. A simple game. Murder in the dark.

(Darkness. The light becomes blue/violet. A violin tunes up.)

CROWLEY: O melancholy brothers, dark, dark, dark.

(The violin plays an eerie music.)

CROWLEY: But if you would not this poor life fulfil,
Lo, you are free to end it when you will,
Without the fear of waking after death.

(Darkness. Tom-toms begin. Dim light comes up on Neuberg dancing wildly to the beat of the drums. Suddenly everything stops, frozen into a tableau.)

JENSEN: It was all very impressive. The drama was divided into seven acts. Man takes his petition to the old gods and none can answer him. There is not one god there who can answer the riddle of Man.

(Tom-toms beat again. Neuberg resumes his dance. Stop.)

JENSEN: What are the gods, of course, but great caricatures of human faults and virtues? The pantheons of Greece and Rome and Egypt can be interpreted as crude efforts to objectify the inhabitants of the interior world. (Taps head.) There is no mystery. All things are explicable in terms of the human mind. The one great secret is this: You are God. The Kingdom of God is within you.

(Tom-tom beat. The dance whirls into a frenzy in the near-darkness. Neuberg flickers like a flame. At the height of the ecstatic whirl, he falls to the floor. Silence. Absolute darkness. A single gunshot. From the dark, a hollow voice...)

CROWLEY: The Cross is deserted. There is no God. There are no Gods.
Do what thou wilt.

(Lights up on Jensen.)

JENSEN: Mr. DeWend Fenton, of the Looking Glass, wrote:
'We leave it to our readers to say whether this is not a blasphemous sect whose proceedings conceivably lend themselves to immorality of the most revolting character. Remember the long periods of complete darkness, remember the dances and the heavy scented atmosphere, the avowed object of which is to produce what Crowley terms an 'ecstasy' - and then say if it is fitting and right that young girls and married women should be allowed to attend such performances under the guise of a new religion.'

CROWLEY: I look upon the Rites as something of a failure on my part. Pearls before swine. The story of my life, it seems. If I had had the most ordinary common sense, I should have got a proper impresario to have it presented in proper surroundings by officers trained in the necessary technique. Had I done so, I might have made an epoch in the drama, by restoring it to its historical importance as a means of arousing the highest religious enthusiasm.

(The light returns to normal. Neuberg is seated.)

JENSEN: If the gods are dead, what is there to be frightened of?

NEUBERG: There are things more terrible than gods.

JENSEN: We circle around. There's something you're not saying. What are we avoiding? Something pulls us in towards itself like a whirlpool. What's there? What terrible thing is at the heart of this? The circle. Tell me about the circle, Victor.

NEUBERG: I can't say!

JENSEN: No harm will come to you. Tell me about the circle. Why are you afraid?

NEUBERG: Trapped in the circle. Lashed to the wheel. It broke through and I was trapped.

JENSEN: I see. Where did this happen?

NEUBERG: Algeria.

JENSEN: Now we come to it. The end in the beginning. Go back there, Victor. Feel the hot dry wind and the scouring sand. The fragile sky. Tell me why you've come here? What are you doing in Algeria?

NEUBERG: We are to penetrate the mysteries of the thirty Aires.

(Egyptian ambience. The drone of mysterious electronics. The male and female acolytes assume slow-motion god-forms as Crowley speaks.)

CROWLEY: The Enochian system of magic was introduced into the world by Dr. John Dee, the court astrologer of Good Queen Bess, the Virgin Monarch. Via the clairvoyant medium of his assistant, Sir Edward Kelley, Dee encountered a number of spirits who dictated messages in a language unknown to man.

NEUBERG: The lost language of the angels. The one true language of man, as spoken before the fall of Babel.

CROWLEY: These messages included nineteen 'Keys', by which a magician might gain entrance into the thirty Aires or Aethyrs. Which is to say, thirty new dimensions of consciousness. Put simply, here was a method by which man could ascend to Godhood. Neuberg and I were to be a modern Dee and Kelley.
See? I can be terribly helpful when I choose.

NEUBERG: Through the desert, day by day. Each day a new Aethyr. Crowley enters them one by one and reports what he sees there.

CROWLEY: In the third Aethyr, I fought and overcame the demon Elee-tzee-peh-seh-peh. Fish-bellied, winged and insect-limbed, he is the spirit of all hidden faults and frailties. Having none of these, I triumphed effortlessly.

NEUBERG: I maintain and update the magical record. His descriptions of the Aethyrs are logged and catalogued in all their purple glory.

CROWLEY: The mighty universal Wheel of Keh-har, the twentieth Aethyr. Wheel of Fortune, turned by Jupiter, the laughing God.

NEUBERG: But something is waiting for us. I can feel it. Something is waiting out there in the endless desert.

CROWLEY: The City of Pyramids in the Fourteenth Aethyr. A sense of infinite darkness and death. Best entered at night.

NEUBERG: He finds it difficult to enter this Fourteenth Aethyr. The veil resists him and we descend from Mount Dal'leh Addin, defeated. Crowley is seized by an impulse which leads him to submit himself to me for the first time. He sees it as a sacrifice of his ego. After that, it becomes easy for him to enter the Aethyr.

CROWLEY: Those who live in this city are like pyramids of dust. Temples of Initiation and tombs also. Whose eyes are sealed up and whose ears are stopped and whose mouths are clenched, who are folded in on themselves.

NEUBERG: His experiences in the Fourteenth Aethyr result in the death of Crowley's human personality. He becomes one of the Secret Chiefs, Masters of the Temple, who must give up his ordinary human existence in order to teach others.

CROWLEY: And here! The Holy City in the eleventh Aethyr. Armoured angels in their thousands. These stand upon towers of iron, eternally vigilant. For this is the final outpost and this fortress guards the universe against Choronzon, the demon of the outermost Abyss.

(Neuberg twists and writhes, trapped and afraid.)

NEUBERG: Choronzon. Choronzon.

(He sings in a cracked voice.)

The Man in the Moon drinks claret,
with Powder-Beef, turnip and carrot.

JENSEN: That name. Who is Choronzon! Victor!

NEUBERG: Not a 'who'. Not even a thing. Not anything.

CROWLEY: I am to cross the Abyss and face Choronzon. I knew it would come to this in the end. I cannot progress until I have conquered the Abyss.

NEUBERG: Night will fall!

JENSEN: Victor, where are you?

NEUBERG: Bou Saada. Grit on the wind. The sun a hammered disc of white hot metal scorching the sands. Lock your doors, doctor. Protect yourself. We have come to the place that has no name.

We leave the town and we walk until we find a valley of fine and level sand. The sun goes down. The breath of the desert is held as the sky goes dark. Even the stars hide their faces! I know this place!

JENSEN: What are you going to do? Victor?

(Crowley is tracing round the circle on the floor.)

NEUBERG: He draws a circle. To protect me. Or to trap me. Catherine on the wheel. He places rocks in a circle and binds it with the names of power. Outside the circle he draws the triangle of manifestation. That's where it will enter into the world. That is the door through which it will come. He is to be the medium and I am to record the operation.

JENSEN: What will come? What happened that night? What did you see?

CROWLEY: First and deadliest of all the powers of evil. That mighty devil Choronzon, Lord of the Abyss. The malignant, incoherent force that cries out for form and manifestation and whose number is three hundred and thirty three.

NEUBERG: I, Frater Omnia Vincam, a Probationer of the A∴A∴, solemnly promise upon my magical honour and swear by Adonai the Angel that guardeth me, that I will defend this magic Circle of Art with thoughts and words and deeds. I promise to threaten with the dagger and command back into the triangle the spirit incontinent if he should try to escape from it; and to strike with the dagger at anything that may seek to enter this Circle, were it in appearance the body of the Seer himself. And I will be exceedingly wary, armed against force and cunning and I will preserve with my life the inviolability of this Circle. Amen. And I will summon my Holy Guardian Angel to witness my oath, the which if I break, may I perish, forsaken of Him. Amen and Amen.

(Jensen, begins to look nervous. He turns to the audience, talking quickly, as though to allay both his and their fears.)

JENSEN: There's nothing to fear here. Elementary symbolism. The circle is one of the most primitive of all signs, recalling everything from the form of the sun and moon to the abstract conception of time as an endless line - a snake devouring its own tail. Implicit in the circle is the idea of the egg and the womb. The embracing confines of the protective uterine cave. The circle also suggests movement, rolling, travelling. We tumble towards the future and nothing can stop us. Unless we, like the magus, become masters of the wheel.

NEUBERG: *(Watching Crowley's preparations.)* We mustn't be afraid. Fear gives it strength and form. It's all the darkness inside us. Inside all of us. The sick poison of fear and ignorance and hatred. These are the bricks and mortar of Choronzon. Every wicked thought, every hateful act, becomes part of that awful demon.

CROWLEY: Now, then, the Seer being entered within the Triangle, let him take the Victims and cut their throats, pouring the blood within the Triangle.

JENSEN: Nothing to fear. Science and common sense will see us through. These things are simply projections of what Doctor Freud calls the subconscious mind. They have no objective value. The triangle, of course, has the attributes of stability and permanence. It recalls the mass and weight of the pyramids, the bulk of mountains. Being of rational disposition, it is only to be expected that we trap our demons within straight lines and angles. These dark intrusions from the cellars of the mind represent all our wayward impulses. How better to contain them than within Euclidean geometry? I am right, aren't I?

NEUBERG: I'm afraid. He's not coming into the circle of protection. What's he doing out there? I mustn't be afraid. Choronzon thrives on fear. If there's a single spark, he'll ignite it to a blaze. *(Deep breaths.)* I'm afraid of nothing.

(He looks at Crowley.)

Nothing.

CROWLEY: I plan be the first magician in history to face the demon on his own ground. I will remain in the triangle of manifestation and allow Choronzon to be present within me.

JENSEN: And if we dare to leave the wheel, what then? Can we halt our blind fall into an unknown future? Do we survive the future by confronting and overcoming its demons here and now?
I can't watch. I must watch.

(Jensen withdraws.)

NEUBERG: This is insane. Someone should stop him.
He takes the pigeons and cuts their throats, letting the blood drain into the sand within the triangle.

(Neuberg looks around wildly.)

Don't leave me, doctor!

CROWLEY: Let not one drop fall without the triangle or else Choronzon shall be able to manifest in the universe.

NEUBERG: Vampire sand laps at the blood. Absorbing all trace. This living blood will form the material foundation from which Choronzon will manufacture a form. What am I to do?

CROWLEY: Defend the Circle. Don't be afraid for me. I'll be in a safe place.

NEUBERG: He draws his hood across his face and recites the Tenth Aire. The Key. The call to bring Choronzon out of the Abyss of nonbeing.
I don't want to be here.
Doctor, where are you? Get me out of this!

(Shrill and hideous, the note of a violin. Crowley is seated cross-legged in the triangle. He bows his head and intones the dreadful prayer.)

CROWLEY: I know you.
I know your name.
I know your incoherent nature.
You are the great Demon,
the Lord of the Abyss,
whose kiss is madness
And whose touch is death.
Yours is the knowledge of Form.
I, Frater Perdurabo, know you
Who sits in the West
Where all things are completed.
By the power of Nee-ah-koh-deh

You will obey me.
Even you, the Archdemon
Will obey my will.

(Tom-toms frantically beating over the above. The shriek of violins and whirr of bullroarers building to a terrible crescendo.
Suddenly silence. The light becomes red.)

CROWLEY: ZODAH-ZODAH-SEH, NAH-ESS-SAH-TAH-NAH-DAH, ZODAH-ZODAH-SEH!

NEUBERG: I can't see him properly. There is someone else there in the triangle. Oh God, help me!

(Crowley's body seems to unfold. He rises slowly, awkwardly. It is as though he is learning to use his muscles for the first time. The effect is disturbing.)

CROWLEY: Victor. Vicky Victor.

JENSEN: Who's there? Who is it you see?

NEUBERG: A woman. I see a woman. A prostitute I knew in Paris. What's happening?

(The female acolyte steps forward, provocative and sensual. Her mouth opens and closes but it is Crowley's voice.)

CROWLEY: Well, well, well. Is that a magic wand in your pocket or are you just pleased to see me?

NEUBERG: Stay back!

(Crowley becomes soppy-sentimental, like a Victorian music hall turn.)

CROWLEY: Is that any way to treat an old friend? It's typical, isn't it? You forgot me but I didn't ever forget you. You came like a thief in the night and you stole my heart away. It was always you, Vicky. Lying there with my legs wrapped round some onion johnny with a striped shirt and bits of garlic stuck between his teeth, it was you I pined for. You and your...baguette.

NEUBERG: Choronzon, I know you!

CROWLEY: I can't believe it! My Victor, my lovely Vicky's a simpering pansy! He's turned you. That terrible Crowley has tried to make you like himself. Those goatish ruttings by candlelight. I know what you really want. I know what you need. A real woman. Like me.
Heavens, it's hot in here! Why don't we slip out of these wet things?
Oh, Victor! I'm in the mood for love.

(The woman attempts to reach into the circle. Neuberg aims his magical knife.)

NEUBERG: I will not be tempted by these ridiculous overtures.

CROWLEY: Not even by a tasty French tart with jam on?

NEUBERG: I know you and I command you to desist!

(The woman retreats into darkness. Crowley comes forward. The entire body language is translated into a new attitude of humility and defeat. An attitude which drips with falseness.)

CROWLEY: Then I am conquered. A sorry demon. Head hung with shame. I have met my master and stand defeated. Let me bow and creep before you, master. Your voice makes the mountains tremble, the winds and the clouds sport at your command. Weathervanes turn, flowers bloom, clocks chime. You float like a butterfly and sting like a bee. You are the perfect master and I am lower than grit. Let me lay my head beneath your conquering foot, humble and contrite, as befits my station. Let me lick the shit of a thousand diabetic camels from the sole of your sandal...

NEUBERG: Stay away! This is an appeal to pride and I will not be swayed.

CROWLEY: Master magus. I simply wish to abase myself before you and to serve you. You have tamed the demon of the Abyss. A feat renowned in history. I am bound in chains at your command. You have only to instruct me and I will fulfil your every desire. Would you like to fly? I can take you from one end of the earth to the other in the blink of an eye. At your command, I can make seas boil and turn winter to summer. I can make you master of nature as you are master of me.

NEUBERG: Be silent.

CROWLEY: Hiroshima, Nagasaki. Master of elements and all material things.

NEUBERG: What?

CROWLEY: I exist only to serve you. Three Mile Island.

NEUBERG: What words are these?

CROWLEY: Chernobyl.

NEUBERG: This is not the word of the Abyss. I order you to reveal the word of the Abyss.

(The male acolyte emerges as an evil old man, back bowed, still circling Neuberg, anticlockwise.)

NEUBERG: His shape changes again. Flesh runs like candlewax and sets.

CROWLEY: The world is ours. Old men with creaking skeletons that shift behind dry skin, eager to be free. The skeleton dance of old men on the graves of the young. We want to bury you all. Our natural home is the graveyard and we will make a cemetery of the world. Dust falls. The death of life. The old men are waiting. Skin splits. Urrrrrrr kkkkkch kkch.

(Crowley becomes a snake.)

NEUBERG: A snake now, like the serpent that tempted Eve. Black and green-veined. Venomous. And sloughs his skin again.

(Becomes Crowley, gasping on the sand.)

CROWLEY: Out. Out. I'm purged of it. Diarrhoeic exit. The demon leaves by the back door. It'll take me days to clean this robe.

(He rises, unsteadily.)

Victor, it's gone. It's over.

(Neuberg is uncertain.)

NEUBERG: But the word. What was the word?

(Crowley lurches forward.)

CROWLEY: Choronzon has gone. I feel hollowed out, apple-cored. I Must have a drink. Water.

NEUBERG: Wait! Don't think I can't see through your deceptions.

CROWLEY: What are you talking about? Please! For God's sake, Victor, I must have water or I'll die in this hideous bloody desert!

NEUBERG: Clothes don't make the man. You dress in his skin but you're not he.

CROWLEY: My death will be on your conscience! Water, you bastard! Water, I beg you!

NEUBERG: No.

(Crowley collapses, changing shape again. He becomes nothing solid. A threatening force now. A dreadful incoherent presence, which radiates unfocussed malice.)

JENSEN: And what then?

NEUBERG: I grow tired of this charade! I charge you in the name of the Most High to abandon deception and reveal thy true nature.

CROWLEY: I spit on the name of the Most High. I am the pox on the face of the Most High. I tear the wings from angels' backs. I shit on the golden throne of Heaven, overturn it and dance in the bloody ruins of Paradise. God and Christ slobber and debase themselves at my feet. I have no fear of the power of the Pentagram, for I am Master of the Triangle. I shall say words and you will write them down, thinking them to be great secrets of magical power. And all the while I will be jesting with you..

NEUBERG: In the name of the mighty angel Aiwass, I demand that you reveal your name and your nature!

CROWLEY: *(Spits.)* Aiwass! Aiwass! I know the name of this Angel and I know that all your dealings with him are no more than the cloak for your filthy sorceries. You hide behind the radiant light but all the while you practise acts of darkness. Sodomites and murderers. The stained sheets of lust will be the shroud that wraps your stinking corpse.

(Neuberg begins to lose confidence.)

NEUBERG: No. You know nothing. My knowledge surpasses yours!

CROWLEY: Only your shame surpasses mine! Will you find the light of heaven up the arse of your false guru? I think not.

NEUBERG: You understand nothing.

CROWLEY: But do you understand...Nothing? What is it you fear?

NEUBERG: *(Guarded, uncertain.)* Nothing.

CROWLEY: Yes. That Abyss from which you called me is where I'll send you when I take your place on Earth. I understand only too well the bestial gruntings and the sweat of your corruption. They are the hooks by which I'll reel you in, twitching like a landed fish. Oh, you've made a terrible mistake bringing me here. Your tainted circle is no protection.

(Neuberg tries to regain control.)

NEUBERG: I command you once more. Declare yourself and give me the word of the Abyss!

CROWLEY: My name is 'Dispersion'. You may talk all night but I cannot be defeated in argument. Try again. Try again ! In the end, I'll break through your useless circle and your life will be mine to lead.

(Slowly, horribly, Crowley begins to hop and creep around the circle. He sings 'Tom O' Bedlam' in a cracked and wavering voice. A voice heard in a nightmare. And as he sings, as he draws Neuberg's attention, he flicks sand across the circle.)

Forth from my far and darksome Cell
Or from the deep Abyss of Hell.
Mad Tom is come to view the world again,
To see if he can ease his distempered brain.
Fear and care doth pierce my soul,
Hark how the angry Furies howl.

NEUBERG: What are you doing? Wait.

CROWLEY: Pluto laughs and Proserpine is glad
To see poor naked Tom of Bedlam mad.

I'm through. I'M THROUGH!

(Crowley becomes a raging beast, breaks into the circle and attacks Neuberg in slow motion. They struggle. Tom-toms, screaming violins. Crowley attempts to tear Neuberg's throat with his teeth. Neuberg drives him back into the triangle. Crowley screams and rages.)

CROWLEY: The torments of Hell await you, you bastard! Glass broken beneath your eyelids!

Vinegar and bile racing through your veins. You'll piss boiling blood and shit splinters.

(Neuberg repairs the circle with his magic dagger. He is almost hysterical now, barely holding onto his self-control. The attack has shaken him terribly. Crowley sits in the triangle, cross-legged.)

NEUBERG: You're a liar. Have you no more shapes to show me? Have you reached the end of your invention?
Well? What else have you to offer?

(Crowley bows his head.)

JENSEN: Victor? Victor, it's time to finish this. There's no need to put you through any more.

NEUBERG: What?

JENSEN: Wake up, Victor! Wake up! It's finished.

(Neuberg is disoriented. He looks around wildly.)

NEUBERG: I have to defend the circle. Choronzon? Where is Choronzon?

JENSEN: There is no Choronzon. There was no Choronzon.

NEUBERG: I fought him. I wrestled with a demon in the form of a naked savage. As Jacob mastered the angel, I overcame the demon.

JENSEN: There was no demon. There was only Crowley. Another of his cruel jests. Initiation by terror. Don't you understand, Victor?

NEUBERG: No. I don't understand. What are you trying to tell me?

JENSEN: The trial by terror, in which the candidate is forced to defend himself against his worst fear. Crowley pretended to be possessed by Choronzon. There was no Choronzon. It was Crowley! He forced you to confront your deepest terrors.

NEUBERG: And I failed. I allowed him to breach the circle I'd sworn to defend. He broke through. Frontiers come down. All is chaos and turmoil. My mind is a painted wall shattering into fragments. I become Choronzon and it becomes me.

JENSEN: The confrontation of the conscious and subconscious minds. There are no demons. There is no magic. There is only the tormented, disturbed mind. You must see that now. You have cursed yourself. Can't you see that I'm right? That wall is the work of your own hands.

NEUBERG: Well, I suppose. Yes.

JENSEN: Crowley is a charlatan, as you have long suspected.

NEUBERG: But what about the things he taught me? What about the visions and the wonders?

JENSEN: Hypnotism. Vaudeville trickery. He overwhelmed you with his personality, deceived you with talk of secrets and enlightenment and for what? So that he could train you as a homosexual partner to satisfy his strong effeminate urges. You have been the victim, not of magic, but of sexual pathology. This is a case for Kraft-Ebbing and not Abra-Melin the Mage.

NEUBERG: It makes sense. I can see how you might come to such a conclusion but I'm still not sure...

JENSEN: Of course, it makes sense! Who ever heard of buggery as a form of magic? Your impressionable nature has made you a perfect victim. Forget Crowley. Forget his talk of Holy Guardian Angels and new Aeons. Cut the chains that bind you. Set yourself free. Your life is your own.

(There is a pause. Neuberg suddenly becomes aware of the figure of Crowley, still seated in the triangle.)

NEUBERG: Doctor Jensen? Who is that there? Who is it that sits so silently there?

JENSEN: What? There's no-one.

NEUBERG: Silence.

JENSEN: What's wrong, Victor? What are you trying to say?

(Neuberg looks directly at Jensen.)

NEUBERG: For Choronzon, in the confusion and chaos of his thought, is much terrified by silence.

JENSEN: Victor, you're allowing yourself to become obsessed by this. Nothing is gained by silence. How am I to help you if you seal your lips?

NEUBERG: And by silence can he be brought to obey...

JENSEN: Talk to me, Victor.

(Neuberg, resolutely silent, stares at Jensen in a confrontational manner.)

Victor, I demand that you talk to me! Remember that my time and expertise costs money! Why waste it in silence?

(Neuberg raises his dagger and points it at Jensen.)

Stop it, Victor!
STOP!

(Jensen covers his face and shrinks back. Slow motion, as though blown back by a terrible slow wind. Crowley rises. Jensen and he stand together, looking at Neuberg.)

NEUBERG: What now?

(Crowley begins to chant sonorously. A children's playground game. Jensen takes up the responses.)

CROWLEY: Call the doctor.

JENSEN: Call the doctor.

CROWLEY: He is ill.

JENSEN: He is ill.

CROWLEY: Call the priest.

JENSEN: Call the priest.

CROWLEY: He is dying.

JENSEN: He is dying.

CROWLEY: Call the undertaker.

JENSEN: Call the undertaker.

CROWLEY: He is dead.

JENSEN: He is dead.

(They approach Neuberg. Ritualistic steps. He looks confused and uncertain.)

NEUBERG: How did it happen?

JENSEN: A poet's death, Victor. A Romantic death. Consumption.

NEUBERG: Oh God. I'd better lie down then, I suppose.

(Neuberg lies down. Jensen and Crowley address the audience.)

CROWLEY: Pathetic. When I met him he was writing feeble verses of hardly more than undergraduate merit. Under my training, he produced some of the most passionate, intense, musical and lofty lyrics in the language.

He left me; the dog hath returned to his vomit again, and the sow that was washed, to her wallowing in the mire. His latest work is as lifeless and limp as it was before I took hold.

Still, we should not protect the weak from the results of their own inferiority. By doing so, we perpetuate the elements of dissolution in our own social body. We should rather aid nature by subjecting every newcomer to the most rigorous tests of his fitness to deal with his environment.

The Book of the Law regards pity as despicable.

JENSEN: In the years following the breakdown of his association with Aleister Crowley, Victor Neuberg was conscripted into the army where he served as a private in the Army Service Corps. According to his sergeant at the time, Neuberg was:

(Crowley, assuming a military tone and bearing picks up the statement.)

CROWLEY: 'Only kept together by string and sealing wax. He could never shave without cutting himself and so he always looked like Death from a Thousand Cuts. He had no manual dexterity.

His movements were not synchronised. His hands and feet worked from two different dynamos. He was the walking mockery of the entire army system and everything it was meant to be.'

(Hysterical laughter from the 'corpse' of Neuberg.)

JENSEN: By 1919, Neuberg had been discharged from the army and went to live at Vine Cottage in Steyning, where he established a small private press to publish his own poetry. His readership was lamentably small. In 1921, he married Kathleen Goddard, who bore him a son and almost immediately afterwards took a lover. According to his friend Hayter Preston:

CROWLEY: 'Victor, at Steyning, was a dead man.'

JENSEN: However, during his time at Steyning, Victor became part of the Sanctuary, a colony of Bohemians, anarchists and freethinkers. He was visited by Tallulah Bankhead, Lord Alfred Douglas and Gertrude Stein, among others.

At the Sanctuary he met the woman who was to be his companion for the remainder of his life and in 1933, he was appointed poetry editor of the Sunday Referee. His weekly poetry competitions unearthed several major talents, including the young Dylan Thomas.

He had a job he enjoyed. He lived with a woman who loved him.

(Crowley smiles wickedly, triumphantly.)

CROWLEY: He died of tuberculosis on May thirty-first, 1940.

JENSEN: Can a man die twice?

CROWLEY: A man can die any number of times, doctor. We must die to be born again. This is the mystery of the Wheel.

(Sound of a gong. Egyptian ambience. The doctor kneels down and begins to mime the mummification of Neuberg's body.)

JENSEN: The mummification process begins with the removal of the viscera. A slit here, from the pelvis to the groin will suffice.

(He makes the incision and reacts with sudden revulsion to what we presume is a hideous smell rising from Neuberg's guts.)

Good heavens! Oh!

(Jensen covers his mouth with his hand.)

NEUBERG: I'm terribly sorry but I'm not a well man, doctor.

JENSEN: Not to worry. I'll just fill the space up with linen and resin. Keeps the pong down to a minimum.
Now, where's my chisel? That brain will have to go.

(Jensen mimes the mummification process - hammering a chisel up into the nose, drawing down the brain with hooks.)

CROWLEY: We see here the mummified body of the age that is passed. Old attitudes, useless dogmas preserved for all time in the glass case of some future museum.

'Was this bandaged thing once worshipped as a god?' the children will ask. 'Was this grotesque mannequin ever taken seriously?'

Of course, it is customary for each new Aeon to begin with a dark age period. The Tamas stage of the Hindu Wheel of Samsara. Don't say I didn't warn you. Living in such an age, it should come as no surprise that sometimes the mummies walk. The tales of terror we find in our penny-dreadfuls and pulp papers are all too horribly true. The mummies not only walk but manage also, to run the affairs of countries. The dead take charge of the living, poisoning the clear waters of the future with their outdated corruption.

JENSEN: Does anyone want the brain? I've had to pull it down through the nose with hooks, so it's somewhat the worse for wear, I'm afraid. What am I to do with the pieces?

CROWLEY: I'd suggest you find some hungry cat, doctor.

JENSEN: Righto!

(Jensen continues. Packing the body cavities with linen and resin.)

CROWLEY: Yes, the mummies walk and will continue to walk until we escape from the Wheel.

Consider those fish, our ancestors, that swam blissfully in the Devonian lakes, 350 million years ago. Adrift in their weightless continuum, how could they have imagined a world of gravity and solidity? And yet, some of those fish were to struggle out of the lakes and onto the land. Breathing air instead of water, crawling instead of swimming, raising their eyes to the hard sky, how could they have turned back and explained to their fellows in the oceans what it was like to evolve?

(Jensen pushes resin plugs into the mouth, nose and ears of Neuberg.)

NEUBERG: Must you seal up my nose and mowfff?

JENSEN: Terribly sorry, old man. I'm only doing my job.

(Wrapping the body.)

CROWLEY: Fish in the waters could not conceive of existence on land, until the drying out of their lakes and pools forced them to adapt to a whole new mode of being. The first great birth trauma of life itself. From those fish came reptiles, birds, early mammals and finally man himself. What will it take to compel humankind to cast aside its chains?

The time is coming when we must dare to leave the water. What we may become is as beyond human conception as the land fish was beyond the conception of his brethren in the seas. The mind is the doorway through which we must enter this new medium of existence and Magick is the method by which we train the mind. No machine will take us there, for machines are simply extensions of our bodies and, as I say, those bodies have almost outlived their usefulness.

My work and the legacy I will leave, involves nothing more than the evolution of the species, in preparation for the fourth Aeon that is to follow the Aeon of Horus. If my Word is ignored, humanity will continue blindly upon the road it mistakes for 'progress' and find at the end of that road a yawning precipice.

How then to avoid that precipice, you say? Well, what do you expect from me? Time and time again, I have pointed to the exit but time and time again, I am asked the same pointless questions.

'Teach us your real secret, Master!' they yap. 'How to become invisible, how to acquire love, and oh! beyond all, how to make gold.'

It's always the same. The real secret is in plain sight but all they want is gold and the Secret of Infinite Riches. Very well then, I will give you the secret. Come closer. Listen.

(Pause.)

CROWLEY: A sucker is born every minute.

(Gong sound. Jensen completes his work and helps Neuberg to his feet.)

JENSEN: The body has been prepared. The soul awaits Judgement.

(Neuberg holds out his arms to Crowley, wrists together.)

NEUBERG: It's a fair cop, guv'nor. Slap on the bracelets.

CROWLEY: The deceased is led out of his body and escorted to the Hall of Two Truths.

(Jensen stands with arms spread, becoming the scales in which the souls of the dead are weighed.)

He is brought through the Doors of the Dead. Osiris leads him to the place of Judgement. Tahoteh, the Scribe sits with reed pen in hand. Anubis, jackal-headed, waits by the scales. In one pan of the scales, there lies a feather. In the other pan, the heart of the deceased is to be placed and weighed against the feather. And there, in the wings...

(He gestures to the audience.)

...waits the many headed monster Am-mit, Eater of the Dead, who will devour the heart-soul of the candidate, if it is found to be heavy with sin. Victor Benjamin Neuberg, you are required to make an account of yourself before this divine tribunal. We want to hear the lot. All your grubby little secrets and furtive sins. Let's hear the verdict on a life of shame.

NEUBERG: I am ashamed of nothing that I've done. My only crime was to have believed that there are leaders worthy of following. And if this is, indeed, a crime then it is the crime of much of humankind. We follow, I followed, simply because we will not take charge of our own destinies. How can we complain then, when we are led into harm? How can we protest when we find ourselves living in that state of moral corruption from which there seems no escape? Ultimately, there is no God but man. There is no wall that was not built by human hands. I'm only sorry I didn't see it when I was alive. It is not enough to paint on the wall, we must tear it down.

I have seen the Great Wheel of Life and Death and I know that it is leaders who turn that Wheel. We permit them to turn it, just as we allow ourselves to be crushed beneath the Wheel of the car of Jaganath. An end to gods! An end to leaders! An end to slavery!

(Bored, Crowley looks at his watch.)

CROWLEY: Yes, yes. We've heard all that. Grubby anarchist gibberish. Quite frankly, we'd all been hoping for something a little more scandalous. It's just as well you died before your life had the opportunity to become even more spectacularly tedious.

NEUBERG: I make a plea for those of us who are merely human and do not aspire to Godhood!

CROWLEY: To be 'merely human' is no longer an acceptable goal. The 'merely human' way has brought the world to the brink of catastrophe. This century of war and chaos is the final expression of what it is to be 'merely human'. Isn't it time we all tried a little harder?
Still, you've said your piece and your time has come. Let's take a look at that heart of yours and see if it counterbalances the feather of Maat.
Open up.

(Reaches 'into' Neuberg's breast to take his heart.)

Oh dear. Nothing there.

NEUBERG: You took my heart a long time ago.

(Crowley reaches into his pocket and withdraws a lump of meat.)

CROWLEY: Well spotted! I did indeed take your heart. It's in here, covered with bits of lint and chocolate crumbs. How mundane you were, Neuberg.

NEUBERG: Better to be mundane than a monster of inhumanity.

CROWLEY: I disagree entirely. But let's see if your heart's really as heavy as you make it sound.

(He places the heart on one of Jensen's palms. The balance tips, the heart is too heavy.)

Oh, dear. The soul-eater snarls and licks his chops! Down boy!

NEUBERG: Wait! There's something stuck there!

(Crowley reaches out and delicately peels a ticket from the heart.)

CROWLEY: Sorry about that. Tram ticket.

(The balance stabilises. Neuberg's heart and the feather weigh the same. A third gongstroke.)

Well done, my boy! Somebody up there likes you and you win a luxury all-expenses-paid trip to the Western Lands! The sun-kissed fertile Fields of Aaru! The sweet meadows of Everlasting Peace!

NEUBERG: It's a dream come true. I don't know what to say.

CROWLEY: Then don't say anything. Silence, after all, is the means by which we vanquish Choronzon.

(Crowley rises, arms wide and is frozen in his triumph. He looks suitably, mockingly beatific, eyes cast heavenward throughout. Jensen and Neuberg look up at him.)

JENSEN: And this then was Aleister Crowley. Poet. Extraordinary chess player. Expert mountaineer. A man vilified and persecuted by the press, who described him as The Wickedest Man in the World.

NEUBERG: A human beast.

JENSEN: A Man we'd Like to Hang.

NEUBERG: A Cannibal at Large.

BOTH: King of Depravity.

CROWLEY: Father, forgive them! They know not what they do.

NEUBERG: Messiah of the New Aeon. The Age of Horus, the Crowned and Conquering Child! Look at you now! I'm not afraid of you! Scarecrow messiah! You don't frighten me. A head full of stuffing and straw! Scarecrow-Crowley. Scarecrowley!
(Neuberg laughs madly.)

JENSEN: He really believed himself to be the Messiah of the new age? Perhaps it's true. God knows, the signs are there. Portents and auguries. The old world fragmenting and assuming new forms. The painting, the music, the poetry, the great engines and lights of a new age. This terrible war in Europe. It's easy to see how these things could be read as the signs of some awful divinity at work.

NEUBERG: Horus, Lord of Force and Fire, Silence and Strength. This war and others to follow were all foretold. In 1904, in Egypt, Crowley was contacted by a praeterhuman intelligence which identified itself as Aiwass. This Aiwass dictated the Book of the Law, the Bible, no less, of the age that would overthrow the old age of Osiris - the dying and resurrected God.

NEUBERG: And if he was the new Messiah, what was my role? What part did I play in the passion play of Saint Aleister Crowley? Was I cowardly Paul at cockcrow? Thomas the Doubter?
Judas?

CROWLEY: How about Mary Magdalene?

(He makes a raunchy pelvic thrust.)

See anything you like, big boy?

NEUBERG: I know for certain that I was the first martyr to his cause.

(Neuberg assumes crucifixion pose.)

CROWLEY: Three great aeons. The watery aeon of Isis first, when the matriarchal powers held sway. The universe was seen as simple nourishment for emergent mankind.
This was followed by the aeon of Osiris. The age of air, when the dying God rose to power. The stern Father, whose law is judgement and

catastrophe.   Osiris, Christ, Attis. All the moribund old farters and the sheep-faced martyrs, pinned to their trees like love notes no-one cares to read anymore.

Now we are entering the fiery Aeon of Horus, the Child, when sin and restriction fall away and we are made innocent again.

For I am Crowley and I come to set mankind free from the chains of the corrupted, corpse-God. The buried God whose smell refuses to go away. I come to set mankind free from the slave gods!

(Crowley turns on Neuberg.)

You! I charge you, the so-called God of Love, of crimes against human evolution! Love? You wouldn't know love if it gave you the clap in a Soho whorehouse! Nine million witches burned in your name! Countless wars fought under your bloody banner! You stand accused of inspiring a lunatic cult which has hindered the cultural development of the entire Western World.

How do you plead?

NEUBERG: *(Simpering Nuremberg tones.)* I was only following orders.

CROWLEY: GUILTY!

I will overthrow you! I will bury your skinny body in an unmarked grave, where it belongs. I will salt the earth and tramp the dirt down. Come forward and fight me like a man.

(Crowley faces Neuberg. They seem to battle with their wills. Blood bursts from Neuberg's mouth and he falls slowly and horribly to his knees, onto his face. Christ cast down. Silence. Red light fades.)

It's over. Crowley has conquered the Abyss.

(The light of Jensen's study returns.)

JENSEN: And was that the end of it?

NEUBERG: We light a fire to purify the area and to destroy all traces of the circle and the triangle. We leave the place and continue our journey through the Arab lands.

I find myself in the care of Doctor Edward Jensen, sweet leech. Together we set out in search of the shattered parts of me. He mesmerises me and takes me back through the years of my association with Aleister Crowley. I meet Crowley and become his disciple. The Paris Workings. The Rites of Eleusis. That dreadful night at Bou Saada. We leave and continue our journey. I find myself in the care of Doctor Edward Jensen who mesmerises me.

The Wheel turns. There is no curse greater than the knowledge that humanity is doomed to repeat its mistakes and never learn from them. Each generation relives the nightmare of the previous one. Each new shining future, glimpsed on the horizon, is tarnished and soiled beyond repair by the time we reach it.

Once I believed in the potential of man. I saw men like angels, crowned with rainbows. I saw

Parádise regained through science and the

Now I see Nothing. I have failed to cross the

Abyss and on every side, all around me, there is

Nothing.

CROWLEY: What are you gibbering about, Neuberg?

NEUBERG: Nothing.

CROWLEY: Typical. And thus we began our delightful
march across Algeria.

*(Crowley teases up the hair on Neuberg's head, to
make horns.)*

CROWLEY: I soon saw that Neuberg with his
shambling gait and erratic gestures, his hangdog
look and his lunatic laugh, would damage me in
the estimation of the natives. So I turned the
liability into an asset by shaving his head except
for two tufts on the temples, which I twisted up
into horns. I was thus able to pass him off as a
demon that I had tamed and trained to serve me
as a familiar spirit.

*(Crowley is terribly pleased with his wit and
invention. Neuberg capers around as the two begin to
move offstage.)*

This greatly enhanced my eminence. The more
eccentric and horrible Neuberg appeared, the
more insanely and grotesquely he behaved, the
more he inspired the inhabitants with respect for

the Magician who had mastered so fantastic and fearful a genie.

(Neuberg laughs hysterically. The laugh pitches upwards into a terrible scream of despair. A moment of silence. Crowley looks at this beaten, wretched creature. Looks up at the audience.)

What a piece of work is a man.

(Lights go down on all but Jensen. Crowley and Neuberg depart.)

JENSEN: Silence is not what it was. In the space between words, I can hear only the thunder of engines, the sound of bombs and men dying. The grinding of iron wheels in black factories. The worst of it is the repetition. It's the heartbeat of the world now.

What spirits are these we have evoked in our search for knowledge and progress? What demons have we set loose? What bargains have been struck and what price must we now pay?

Babel is fallen. It's true. All words lose their meaning. All signs are empty signs. We stand amidst ruins. Ruins of ideologies, ruins of systems, ruins of men and women, like Victor Neuberg.

And here am I in the dark with the pieces in my hands. What am I to do? What is the way forward?

Ultimately, what is left but to sit like a penitent monk who has lost his faith, alone in the gathering night, turning my prayer wheel and waiting in vain for some voice in the darkness?

(Lights go out on Jensen. Crowley returns, standing in the circle, facing the audience).

CROWLEY: But to love me is better than all things: if under the night-stars in the desert thou presently burnest mine incense before me, invoking me with a pure heart, and the Serpent flame therein, thou shalt come a little to lie in my bosom. I love you! I yearn to you! Pale or purple, veiled or voluptuous, I who am all pleasure and purple, and drunkenness of the innermost sense desire you.
Put on the wings and arouse the coiled splendour within you! Come unto me!

(He throws wide his arms, triumphant.)

CROWLEY: EVERY MAN AND WOMAN IS A STAR!

(Tom-toms beat a final, furious tattoo. The lights go out.)

I'M A POLICEMAN

"How about a newly-born baby with 'Fuck me! It's Diet Cloke!' felt-tipped on its tit?" Di yells. "Sort of like a message from God, you know? The way people keep finding the name of Allah when they cut marrows in half..."

"Benetton did that one ages ago," I mutter.

I know she can't hear me; the party's beginning to peak now as the nation's hippest young band take to the stage and launch into their Christmas number one 'A Binary Precursor for SN 1987A?'.   Already the anthem of a generation, the song is the first to openly hint at an explanation for the curiously axisymmetric rings of Supernova 1987A. The group, *Microbiology In Clinical Practice*, are two girls, two boys, a gender transient and a dog; it's an almost perfect blend and their brand of *'Hexstasy-fuelled Concrete Jungle has defined the 'commence de siecle'* (sic) spirit of a post-techno generation desperate to throw off the oppressive shackles of hand-me-down baggy psychedelia in the wake of the murder of the Moon Goddess by the Sun King, which signalled, as did the American moon landing in 1969, an attempt by rigidly patriarchal power structures to regain control over an increasingly fluid and feminine tendency in Western art and culture ....(as I wrote in the liner notes for their debut CD/ROM 'Hello Boys', the cover of which features a starving Rwandan waif holding two crudely-carved begging bowls at chest height) .

I decide to go out onto the balcony. I feel like playing with my gun. As I emerge into the cryogenic chill from the colossal storm of light particles and sound waves that is the Party, a Nuremberg-style cheer goes up. A millions-strong human traffic jam, stretching all the way back down the Mall, bubbles and ripples like the surface of the archaic tar pits which once consumed the dinosaurs.

THEY COULDN'T GO BACK TO SCHOOL

We've been trying to think of ways to market Cloaca-Cola, the arriviste soft-drink sensation from the newly-emerging economic superstate that is the Indian sub-continent. Cloke derives its piquant and surprising aftertaste from an infusion of ashes; the by-product of burning tonnes of human excrement in huge cremation pyres.

Citing the great Tantric masters, Cloke bosses are selling their product on the proven health and longevity benefits of consuming powdered human faeces.

"I'm thinking we should keep it simple," I say.

Di weaves through the Jarmanesque turmoil of dancing clergymen, defrocked coppers and exotic Go-Go Girl Guides, trailing clouds of 'Conformity' by Calvin Klein (a fragrance so potent it's almost visible). Four hundred miles away, dogs in Scotland smell her coming and whimper in their sleep.

PLENTY OF EXCITEMENT

"I'm the country's greatest living writer, for fuck's sake! My ad campaigns are mainstays of the Sixth Year Studies English Curriculum! Why am I having deadline trouble with this Cloke gig?" No-one answers.

All I need is a slogan. The clock runs out at midnight. If I don't modem the goods to New Delhi by then, the shit flies like 'Challenger' flew: I blow the biggest publicity coup of all time. I've decided to make them sweat a little. I swing my leg over the balcony and get comfy before taking aim. The motion of the crowd simulates peristalsis.

"Starorzewski! Starorzewski !" They cry with one voice, spotting me. Relenting for a moment, I cradle the rifle in my lap and lift a bright red megaphone to my lips. Words shall be my weapons.

"YOU'RE ALL BEING DUPED BY THE CAPITALIST MEDIA MACHINE!" I scream.

"FORCE-FED A DIET OF OTHER PEOPLE'S LIVES, YOU SIT CHAINED TO YOUR TELEVISION SETS, AVIDLY CONSUMING THE LATEST MEANINGLESS FICTIONS WHILE YOUR OWN DEVALUED EXISTENCES ARE CONDENSED INTO MINUTE-LONG 'VIDEO NATION' CLIPS ON BBC 2! LET TEN MEN AND WOMEN MEET WHO ARE RESOLVED ON THE LIGHTNING OF VIOLENCE RATHER THAN THE AGONY OF SURVIVAL; FROM THIS MOMENT DESPAIR ENDS AND TACTICS BEGIN!"

The crowd cheers and the sound is like an avalanche of bass drums. I swiftly snatch up the gun, discouraged, and glue my eye to the scope. Caught in the precision crosshairs of my telescopic sight, a hysterically-haemorrhaging novice nun moulds a life size photograph of my face to the contours of her own and forces her tongue through my unsmiling lips.

Now I've seen everything.

A NICE EVENING'S WORK

"They can't hear a word you're saying," Di tells me, lounging into view stage left. "Christ! It's freezing out here!"

She's right but I don't care. I'm generating Tummo, the psychic heat of the Tibetan Lamas. Far from being cold, I'm producing enough thermal energy to light a cigarette.

"Every word you say is being monitored and electronically detourned by MI6 Anti-Situationists, using negative sound technology," Di goes on, baiting me. (The French bio-terrorist cell that hothouse-cloned her from a stain on the blacktop created a monster.)

"Nothing you just came out with has anything to do with what they hear.""

"I love Big Brother."

"Me too."

I can see Di's wearing contact lenses with 3-element multi-coated air-spaced optics, which allow her to see far beyond the range of the naked eye.

"You're missing all the fun, you know," she says. Her lenses whirr as they zoom in on the crowd. "They're waiting for the End of the World. In fifteen minutes, the 90's will be over. It'll all be over. For them anyway."

"I love technology," I say with genuine feeling, and look back into the huge stateroom where the last and greatest party of the Age of Pisces is in full swing.

ALL GOOD THINGS END !

On screen are some of Di's latest "Hello!" photospreads blown up to epic, Hitlerian proportions: Here, in a Rei Kawabuko tank dress, daintily regurgitating a tiny roasted quail into the chirping open mouth of her eldest son. Here, artlessly toasting her ex with champagne at 7gs in a Nasa centrifuge. Here again, glittering, nailed to a spinning atom in the simulated crucifixion which ended her run as Unified

Field Theory in Andrew Lloyd Webber's musical adaptation of Stephen Hawking's best-selling '*A Brief History of Time*'. And here - the money shot - Di stripped to the waist, passionately French-kissing a terminal AIDS patient in Bangkok.

"You don't think they're too much?" she asks nervously.

"You look gorgeous darling!" I say.

"Even the one of me shitting on Mother Theresa's grave?"

"It's a fucking masterpiece," I assure her, "Lichfield outdid himself."

"You think so?" she says, brightening. I can always win her over.

"Of course," I say. "I mean, let's face it, at least it's not..." I don't have to say another word. We both smile, recalling Tamara Beckwith's ill-advised photo-diary record of her participation in a pro-celebrity baby seal cull organised by the Norwegian Minster for Culture and his son.

"I know what you mean," Di says, spoiling the moment.

DOWN THE SECRET PASSAGE IN THE MIDDLE OF THE NIGHT

Resuming my telescopic scan of the record-breaking crowd, I try to imagine it as seen from one of the or orbital paparazzi satellites which constantly supply the tabloids with pictures of Di, myself and our dazzling army of human refuse. Seen from a geo-synchronous orbit, 22, 300 miles out into space, the surging biomass might appear as a grotesque cephalopod, jammed uncomfortably into the streets of London. How quickly surveillance surrenders to surrealism! I hover on the brink of epiphany then resight, targeting a dwarf in a red coat, exactly like the one from 'Don't Look Now'.

A WONDERFUL DAY

As though somehow reading my mind, Di has activated the random channel surfer. The Phillips Liquid Crystal Wallpaper display flutters madly, presenting horrific images from Autumn's Paris collections. Top marks for a refusal to compromise with even the basic tenets of civilised society have to be awarded to the Neo-Anti-Nazi Radical Animal Rights designer 'Klaus Shreck', who set the seal on his status as the enfant terrible of the international rag trade when he sent uberwaif Little Nikita down the catwalk wearing the expertly-flayed skin of Naomi Campbell as a pair of culottes. 'Shreck' in that one shocking photo-opportunity was immediately exposed as the international terrorist and sadistic serial killer, 'Leatherneck'. Seized by the police of five countries, amid the popping of champagne corks and flashbulbs, he jeered at reporters, vowing he'd be back to highlight further animal rights abuses.

Little Nikita, after claiming "I was so high on Hex I could have been fucking a giant ant for all I know," was released on bail, wearing a mirror latex spray-on catsuit. Everyone felt sorry for her; Steven Meisel's groundbreaking PET scan shots of her brain in the preceding May's 'Vogue' had resulted in a fashion-conscious doctor's timely identification of the early stages of Creudzfelt-Jakob Disease.

"Can't we have the adverts on?" I whine.

HITCH-HIKING ALL THE WAY

"This is my favourite!" Di says, pointing at the screen.

I snake through the crowd with my scope. The negative Union Jack is everywhere. It feels like Altamont.

I feel like the Omega Man.

"Is this what it's come to?" I muse bitterly through the megaphone.

NIGHT OF SURPRISES

When I look back from my reverie, Di's laughing loudly.

"What's it an advert for?"

"Instant coffee," she says, searching in her purse for the two pink DMT capsules she knows she put there last night.

"It's that new coffee, made from South American holly. It's got five times the caffeine so you have to vomit it up as soon as you've drunk it."

I'm watching a Doberman 'devil dog' savaging ET. The terrified alien's blood splatters the screen with explosive ferocity. It's no contest; the innocent visitor from a gentler world is rapidly pawed and chewed to a bloody psychedelic mess in hi-fidelity slo-mo detail.

With mingled nausea and fascination I stare, entranced. I'm captivated by the director's pornographic fascination with the little alien's viscera, which seem in shamanic fashion to actually spell out the name of the coffee product. I can't bear to look away as CGI technology contrives to put the viewer directly into the action through the fear-maddened eyes of the slavering canine. The whole thing arouses deep sullen electricity in my reptile backbrain. I long to fuck, to defecate, to protect my territory .

"I'm sure these adverts are designed to provoke aggressive territorial responses," I say.

No-one dares contradict me.

THE WARNING OF THE BELLS

The merciless stars shine down. Quasar transmissions from the distant Lyman-Alpha clouds on the rim of the observable universe seem to mock me.

I run the Remington over my skull. Black plastic jacket. 'Smart Thug' T-shirt. Bunker boots. I look like a 'Sweeney' villain.

I look the part.

I've got minutes to go. My PocketMac, with its 64 billion K data storage capacity, (not forgetting the adjustable holographic display, voice-activated virtual mouse and liquid disk drive), is in my hand. I flip open the case and activate the encrypted display with the foolproof password, "I'm just a lousy no-good faggot."

"I'M OKAY! YOU'RE NOT OKAY!" I chant, remembering the joys of the loudhailer for a moment.

GRANDAD'S OLD BOX

On the wall some typically gorgeous pre-op TS in a Vivienne Westwood is wanking across the windscreen of a car while a man drives it into a truck filled with United Nations peacekeeping troops. Something about the scenario is oddly moving; I feel that I've really come to know these people and as the ad ends, I suddenly miss them; the outwardly tough but deeply sensitive and vulnerable she-male; the young soldiers, nervously exchanging jokes and fags in the face of their own mortality; and, perhaps most poignant of all, the ambiguous figure of the driver, hurled into a world he could never hope to comprehend. It all seems so cruel, so far from the bucolic idylls of Papa and Nicole in the timeless Renault Clio series.

"It's for the new Honda Cursor," Di yells.

"It's a fucking award-winner," I whisper, dabbing at my eyes. "I was there. It was like the end of 'Death in Venice'."

A GREAT DEAL OF NEWS

I tap a few words on the Mac screen. It looks promising. I can helicopter rotors now as ten HH-GOA Desert Hawks arrive to airlift the 24-Hour Party guests out to the next location.

MTV's got Nip-Hop band Octylcyanoacrylate, articulating the rage and frustration of middle management white collar salarymen in the compu-software sales division of a Tokyo-based multinational. Somehow we've heard it all before. I fire a shot into the crowd and nobody seems to mind. Gamely, somebody shoots back and takes a chunk out of my shoulder with a semi-jacketed hollow point shell.

"I'm thinking of brain surgery," I say laconically, to mask the dreadful pain of cauterised flesh, chipped bone (although I'm only bringing up the subject to get Di horny, I have been considering a discreet visit to one of the new cosmetic neuro-surgery clinics).

"I thought maybe get some prefrontal cortex work done; you know what my memory's like. Then maybe I could get them to take a look at my IQ. It's big but it's not as big as I'd like."

THE TIME GOES BY

"Eastenders" is on the wall now and Grant Mitchell is having a shockingly convincing nervous breakdown. He's just turned on his telly at 8pm on a Thursday and seen himself watching himself, infinitely regressing. Tiffany arrives at the door, anxious to make up, eager to tell him she's thought of a name for their latest - *Conjunctivitis Associated With Methicillin-Resistant Staphyloccoccus Aureus In A Long-Term Care Facility*, after her granddad - but Grant's gone, his mind folded up and put away like a game of draughts.

Tiff walks into the living room to find him sobbing, in existential crisis. Synth drums sound the crack of doom. The band are coming to the end of their set with the storming, anthemic 'I'm A Policeman'.

Di uses the International Sign Language for the Deaf to tell me that it's time to go.

ALL VERY PECULIAR

Helicopters are beginning to land in the courtyard. The changing of the guard is performed swiftly and with extreme prejudice.

On the wall now, unseen by anyone as the stateroom empties counter-clockwise down the stairs, a veteran comedian is performing a routine in front of a silent audience of men and women wearing cut-out masks of the 'Big Brother' face from the BBC television version of '1984', starring Peter Cushing. The entertainer's nerve is beginning to crack after three televised hours of this terrifying psychological ordeal. He's exhausted his supply of jokes and impressions and is now tearfully confessing to a series of shocking assaults on old age pensioners which he'd carried out a few years ago to help make ends meet between series.

"It's pulling 18 million viewers a week," Di tells me on the way the helicopters.

IN THE MORNING WHAT MORE COULD ANYONE WANT?

We sail up over the cheering crowd, swooping in low over the Palace gates. Everything goes into drifting slow motion. They're playing Di's song, the finale of Elgar's Variations on an Original Theme ('Enigma'). The crowd breaks like a wave against the railings, mouths opening and closing with no sound. Dozens are trampled as we glide overhead and strobe spotlights transform the mall into a grand guignol disco. I reach for my megaphone in an attempt to comfort the bereaved and dying but it's too late. These choppers move fast.

Di has her contacts trained on the palace as it recedes into classical perspective. Our successors, a group of identically-dressed children with white hair and luminous eyes, stand waving on the balcony. I can feel the telekinetic gravity of their unearthly minds, even from here.

"I'm sure they'll do a brilliant job," I say.

ALONG COMES AN ADVENTURE

The helicopters swing like bells as elite Delta-force commandos begin to dance with demented partygoers.

Overhead I can hear the thrumming engines of the fluorescent saffron B-29 bomber the Cloaca-Cola Corporation has chartered for the century's grand finale. "I can't wait to get to New York!" Di shouts, happily, placing a smoking pink capsule on her tongue.

"By the time we've finished there, it'll look like the end of 'Planet of the Apes'! "

HEADLONG INTO TROUBLE

On the portable telly I brought, just in case, the end credits of *'Rape, She Wrote'* are fading on a tinkled harpsichord riff. A little Channel O logo yaps six tones and then all is still.

Bees buzz, idly labouring. Deep summer in the Home Counties. An elderly man is sitting in an idyllic English country garden. He could almost be Sir John Betjeman or perhaps Benny Hill, if Benny had lived. He glances skyward, his geriatric features briefly eclipsed by an uncanny, scalloped shadow.

In a quavering voice he begins:
"I'm terribly sure it's not England;
Those churches look awfully strange.
And...Dear God Almighty!
Some chap in a nightie's
been strung from the spire of the Grange.

"I'm terribly sure it's not England;
The archbishop's fucking the Dean.
And Hitler's delighted,
for Churchill's been sighted,
defiling a child on the Green..."

Off camera, we hear barked commands and the sounds of a firing squad taking aim.

"I've got it!" I say. "Put me through to India!"

Big Ben is gonging the closing seconds of the last thousand years.

ALL GOOD THINGS END!

We're on every channel in the world and thanks to negative sound broadcasts, everyone will hear exactly what they want to hear.

Di hands me a mike, connected to massive Bose speakers mounted to the chopper's fuselage. She's fucked on Hexstasy but she'll be fine in five minutes. High above the fragile cirrostratus layer, the bomb-bay doors of the B-29 flap open. A thousand gallons of Cloaca-Cola rain down from the upper atmosphere in glorious, biblical torrents.

"NEW DIET CLOKE!" I scream, shattering windows.

"FOR PEOPLE WHO WON'T JUST SWALLOW ANY OLD SHIT!"

They're cheering and dancing in the streets. Airborne cameras swoop and dive. Everyone's an extra in the greatest ad of all time.

MAROONED BESIDE THE WHIRLPOOL.

The choppers swing around over the oil-fires and the burning wicker men, bisecting the meridian line at Greenwich, heading West with the new millennium. All over London, Cloaca-Cola is crystallising in the cold air and falling exactly like the snow at the end of that film 'The Dead'.

You have just read "Lovely Biscuits" by Grant Morrison, the first in a series of books which we hope will help launch a revival of imaginative and powerful SF and Horror Fantasy and make the world a weirder place to live in.

You may be interested in the following titles;-

METAL SUSHI by David Conway
(QUANTUM PSYCHOSIS AND HOLOCAUST THEORY)
Enter a world of metamorphic delirium, millennial depravity and misanthropic carnage. Like a hybrid monstrosity spawned from an unholy union between William Burroughs, Ignatius Loyola and the Marquis de Sade, David Conway's stories will take you to a dimension of absolute nightmare.

In 'Eloise' a scientist's obsessions with genetic experiments, coupled with an incestuous relationship, create the New Race.

In 'Manta Red' reality is warped through the Zen Continuum in a crescendo of designer carnage and biological transformation.

In 'Metal Sushi' hermaphrodite/ amphibian detective Satori Thule battles an inhuman racial supremacist cult, with unforeseen consequences.

In 'Black Static' Lovecraftian entities are warped through hyperspace to merge with human destiny in a tale that could be described as 'quantum physics mythos'.

Plus others...

"Conway's combination of superheated, superdense prose.. seems made to be snorted rather than read...the most powerful and distinctive writer of horror fiction since Clive Barker made his debut a decade ago.."
(from the introduction by Grant Morrison)

ISBN 1 902197 00 3
UK: £7.95
US: $12.95

<u>(FORTHCOMING - AUTUMN 1998)</u>

THE HAUNTER OF THE DARK
(and other grotesque visions)
graphic novel adaptations by John Coulthart
Black and white adaptations of H P Lovecraft's tales "The
Haunter Of The Dark" and "The Call Of Cthulhu" plus extracts
from the forthcoming "Dunwich Horror" and a portfolio of
Lovecraft-inspired artwork.

We also intend publishing works by the following authors;-

Alan Moore
Stephen Sennitt
Mike Butterworth
and others.

We will hopefully also release music CDs, which will be an
extension of our vision of how we'd like to see things become.

If you want to be on our mailing list, write to the following
address;

ONEIROS,
8, SHORT STREET,
MOUNT PLEASANT,
SWANSEA
SA1 6YG

MIDIAN BOOKS
Disseminating esoterica since 1991

The best in new and secondhand books on fringe culture. Three catalogues available:

CEASE TO EXIST
New titles. Apocalypse Culture, True Crime, Occult, Sexuality, Cinema, Deviant Art and the best in Transgressive fiction. Latest titles from Amok, Blast, Feral House, Oneiros. Also stocking new issues of Headpress, Funeral Party and related journals. NOW AVAILABLE! The Midian Mailer is an update to the Cease To Exist catalogue, which includes exclusive reviews, art, articles and fiction. Free of charge!

MIDIAN
Secondhand and collectable books on Chaos Magick, Crowley, Secret Societies, Conspiracy Theories, Punishment and Death, Primitive Exotica, Drug Literature, Freaks, Psychotronic cinema and bizarre fiction.

EROTICA
Over 18s only. Contemporary erotica in words and images. Taschen, Creation, adult cinema etc.

For a complete catalogue pack, please send 2 x 26p stamps, 3 I.R.C.s or $3 to:

MIDIAN BOOKS
69 PARK LANE
BONEHILL
NR. TAMWORTH
STAFFORDSHIRE
B78 3HZ
ENGLAND

TEL/FAX: (01827) 281391
EMAIL: enquiries@midian-books.demon.co.uk

THE EDGE

new fiction, in-depth interviews
and detailed reviews

Fiction by
Keith Brooke, Eric Brown, Ramsey Campbell,
Mark Chadbourn, Simon Clark, Paul Di Filippo,
Christopher Fowler, Garry Kilworth, Michael Moorcock,
Kim Newman, John Shirley, Iain Sinclair, Don Webb, Peter Whitehead

Interviews
Anne Billson, Mark Chadbourn,
Storm Constantine, William Gibson,
M. John Harrison, Michael Moorcock, Alan Moore,
Nicholas Royle, James Sallis, Iain Sinclair, Peter Whitehead

And in each issue
Christopher Fowler's column,
David Britton & Kris Guidio's *La Squab* strip,
substantial film, video, book & comic reviews, articles, letters

Bimonthly, 48 A4 pages, colour covers

111 Guinness Buildings
Fulham Palace Road
London W6 8BQ UK

The Edge is available from a variety of small retail outlets or by mail order at £2.50/$6.00 (US); subscriptions £8.00/$20.00 for four issues.

Overseas rates: pay UK prices by International Money Order or Eurocheque, or in US dollars (cash or US checks welcome). All copies sent post free, all overseas orders sent by air mail. Please make cheques, etc, payable to 'The Edge'.

We pay a good rate for our fiction/non-fiction, are always reading, and reply within 3 weeks. Detailed writers guidelines available on request – UK send sae; Europe 1 IRC; outside Europe 2 IRCs or $2 cash. All enquiries as above or tel. (0181) 741 7757 weekdays.